With two soft *splats* a pair of magic spiders landed.

Immediately, both began spinning out strands of glowing silk that floated through the air until they touched another surface. As the webs grew, the strands thickened and became ropy. Salem realized that if he didn't make it up the stairs in about five seconds, the entire foyer would be draped in spiderweb and he'd be caught.

"Icky stickies!" Gotham the dog cried in horror. The threat of danger suddenly filled him with the urge to rescue something. He rolled over and, grasping the scruff of Salem's neck gently but firmly in his jaws, bounded up the stairs, taking them two at a leap. At the top he hurtled toward the open linen closet.

Hanging by his scruff, Salem barely had an idea of what was going on, except that his life was going into the Dumpster and it was all Gotham's fault.

His last memory was of rushing toward the stacked linens. Then there was thunder, a flash . . .

. . . then Nothing.

Titles in SABRINA, THE TEENAGE WITCH™ Pocket Books series:

All Pocket Book titles are available by post from:
Simon & Schuster Cash Sales, P.O. Box 29, Douglas, Isle of Man IM99 1BQ
Credit cards accepted. Please telephone 01624 836000,
Fax 01624 670923, Internet http://www.bookpost.co.uk
or email: bookshop@enterprise.net for details

Sabrina The Teenage Witch™

Go Fetch!

David Cody Weiss & Bobbi JG Weiss

POCKET
BOOKS

LONDON · SYDNEY · NEW YORK · TOKYO · SINGAPORE · TORONTO

POCKET
B O O K S

An imprint of Simon & Schuster UK Ltd
Africa House, 64-78 Kingsway
London WC2B 6AH

A CIP catalogue record for this book is
available from the British Library

ISBN 0 671 02915 0

5 7 9 10 8 6

Printed by Omnia Books Ltd, Glasgow

To JtBoD at the BK
Genuine Soul Food

Go Fetch!

Chapter 1

Salem peered cautiously over the top step onto the second-floor landing. The coast seemed clear, but it was seven A.M., after all. A cat who attempted to carelessly cross that space at this time of the morning could rapidly become a bundle of bruises.

He carefully gauged the distance between the step and the top of the wicker hamper in front of the linen closet. The hamper was risky territory, but at least it was off the ground. He had complete faith in the accuracy of his eyes and reflexes, but in a house with three witches, that wasn't always enough. Salem tensed his muscles, gathering power and focus for the leap. He launched himself through space, aiming for the dead center of the hamper lid.

But magic is quicker than the eye. While he was in midleap the lid popped open. No amount of claw thrashing and backpedaling could keep Salem from clearing the rim and plummeting down into dirty laundry. An instant later, damp bath towels dropped on top of him. "Hey! Have some consideration for the cat, will ya?" he yowled in outrage.

The towels lifted, arcing gracefully through the air to balance several inches above Zelda Spellman's right index finger. Steam rose from her bathrobe into the cool morning air, but her voice held no warmth at all. "Salem! You know better than to get in the way when we're all hurrying!" she barked. "Now get out of there!"

Salem leaped up onto the stair post, narrowly avoiding the damp towels that again flew past and into the hamper. "Huh!" grunted the cat. "I come up to find out why my breakfast isn't ready and get treated like dirty laundry." His fur twitched in irritation.

But the elder Spellman sister was already disappearing back into her own bedroom. In the same instant the door across from Salem was wrenched open and Sabrina lurched out and across the landing, bleary-eyed, irritable, and groping her way toward the bathroom. A moment before she reached the doorway she was rudely cut off by her other aunt, who lunged in ahead of her and tried to close the door.

Sabrina threw her shoulder against it and moaned, "Hey! No fair, Aunt Hilda. You have your own bathroom. I'm going to be late for school."

Hilda countered Sabrina's push, slowly forcing the door closed. "I just need to put on a face," she wheedled through the narrowing gap. "You know that the mirror in mine is broken."

Sabrina wedged her foot into the doorway before the gap closed. *"You* were the one who broke it."

Hilda put her hip into the return thrust. "Well, I didn't like the things it said. It had a bad attitude."

"Never, ever, *ever* ask a magic mirror, 'Do I look fat in this dress?' dear," cooed Zelda as she glided out onto the landing. She was done up in a crisp wool suit and was zipping closed the nylon bag holding her laptop. Her makeup was flawless.

Hilda's eyes widened in surprise and she lost her grip on the door. The sudden lack of resistance threw Sabrina off balance and she toppled forward. "You went and got a custom makeup spell!" Hilda huffed jealously at Zelda.

Sabrina landed on the plush bath mat, and Hilda, oblivious, simply stepped over her so she could scrutinize her sister's face more closely. Sabrina seized the advantage, crawling past Hilda and feebly kicking the door shut. It bumped into Hilda, but she was too busy glaring at Zelda to notice.

"Designer or off-the-looking-glass?" she demanded, automatically preventing the door from shutting with her body.

Zelda purred. "It's an Arkham House Lovecraft Exclusive."

Hilda was so stunned that she let Sabrina gain an inch. "Those things go for unspeakable prices!"

Zelda looked smug and schoolgirlish. "One of my stocks split three for one and I was so giddy that I did something completely unprecedented—I bought myself a present to celebrate."

"Maybe I should start bringing in the mail—especially those dividend statements," Hilda chirped brightly. "Who knows? *I* might get a present."

"And how might that happen?" asked her sister dryly.

Hilda flashed a winning smile. "Oh, I dunno. Enthusiasm fallout, maybe?"

From over on the stair post, Salem's "I'll take a present—breakfast!" drew no notice. He grumbled, "Why do I get the feeling that I'm suddenly invisible? Or not here at all? I could probably be gone for days and not be missed until winter set in and one of you missed my body warmth on the bed at night."

Zelda was staring imperiously at her sister. "Look, Hilda, I haven't got time to make you grovel properly. I have an early chemistry lecture to attend." But even as she spoke, she averted her eyes and some color rose beneath her exquisite makeup.

"Yes, a lecture given by a certain university professor someone's been dating without filling me in," shot Hilda. "Me, her closest relative and friend, who has to look at the calendar to remember what a date *is.*"

4

"Your lack of a love life is your own affair," Zelda replied. She shouldered the laptop case. "Now, if you'll excuse me, I don't want to be late."

Salem pawed at empty air as she breezed down the stairs. "What about my breakfast?" he called after her. His tail cut the air angrily. "Is somebody going to feed the cat?"

Hilda looked from Salem to the bathroom door. She called sweetly to Sabrina. "Oh, Sabrina, your cat needs you!"

Still half asleep, Sabrina fell for it. She let go of the door and leaned into the hallway to ask, "Can't it wait until I've had my shower?"

Hilda took her chance. She strong-armed past Sabrina and closed the bathroom door with a loud slam. The soft *snick* of the lock echoed in the landing. Sabrina glared from the cat to the door and back again.

"Since you're not doing anything at the moment," Salem drawled into the silence, "why don't you go down to the kitchen and fix me a nice canned breakfast? Microwaved to body temperature, of course. We cats like to reminisce about the spoils of the hunt."

"Like you ever hunted anything besides leftovers," snarled Sabrina. She glared back at the bathroom door. "If *I* can't get what I want, why should *you?*"

"That's a rather hostile attitude to take," said

Salem in mock shock. "You know, if *everybody* had that kind of attitude—"

"They'd be just like cats!" Sabrina finished for him.

"Can you think of a better role model?" smirked Salem.

Three sharp raps sounded on the inner surface of the linen closet door.

Salem and Sabrina looked blankly at each other. The knocking came again.

"I couldn't open it even if I could reach it," said Salem, flexing a paw at Sabrina. "That means you get to answer it."

Sabrina tightened the belt on her blue terrycloth robe and stalked over to the door. If it was another closet-to-closet used grimoire salesman again, he was going to get an earful.

The man standing in the linen closet was anything but a salesman. He was tall and rangy, his young face almost handsome in a craggy, weathered sort of way. He wore a heavy tan trenchcoat, belted, with the collar turned up to meet a battered fedora. His hands were jammed deep into the coat's pockets, and the brown oxfords that peeped out from under slightly frayed trousers had seen more miles than good days. His slash of a mouth sprouted a short twig slung like a toothpick in its far corner. He stared flatly at Sabrina through deep-set, liquid eyes for a beat and then rasped, "This the legal residence of Salem Saberhagen?"

To Sabrina's surprise, Salem snorted in derision. "Well, well, well, if it isn't Sam Spayed."

The stranger shot a withering look toward the cat. "The name's Noir, kit. Pet Noir, as if you didn't remember."

"I remember that coat looking a lot better than it does now. Must be pretty slim pickings in the kibble bowl nowadays."

"Your coat is new, I see. Fur, too. Fits you pretty good, considering all the hot air it's gotta hold in."

"On me, fur looks good. You didn't change at all. Once a hound, always a hound."

"You got a thing against dogs, cat?"

"Beyond the stereotypical belief that dogs are stupid, sloppy, and haven't a shred of self-respect? Yes. They stink, too." Salem nodded sagely. "Never met a dog that didn't need a bath."

Sabrina listened to all this as if she were a spectator at a Ping-Pong match. When she got dizzy from looking back and forth so much, she held up her hands, curtly waving for silence. "Will the two of you cork the testosterone long enough to tell me what's going on?"

Pet Noir's half-lidded brown eyes regarded her for a moment. "It's about a guy named Gotham. Used to be a pal of your kitty's."

"He was no pal, he was a lackey," corrected Salem. "He was the kind of guy who needed refresher courses for his refresher courses. Anyway, he hasn't been here. I haven't seen him since I was sentenced to being a cat, and my parole officer will back me up."

"What do you want this guy for?" Sabrina asked Noir.

"Let's just say I want him to answer a couple of questions." Noir didn't speak so much as drawl, cocking his head just enough to give the impression that his simple inquiry was only the tip of a vastly intriguing iceberg.

"A couple of answers? Hah!" Salem laughed. "That's all you'll get from that bozo. By the third question he'll have forgotten his own name."

"He came in pretty handy in your little plan to take over the world, though, didn't he?"

"Someone had to go for pizza," Salem shot back. "Believe me, the last thing in the world I'd want is to see *that* ninny again." He began to groom himself.

Noir snuffled the air deeply, alarming Sabrina. "I've got your scent, cat. I'll take your word now, but believe me—if you're involved in this caper, I'll be on your tail like an old coon dog. And you know I can do it."

He turned to Sabrina and tugged at the rim of his fedora. "Sorry to take up your time, ma'am." He handed her a creased business card. "If anything turns up that you think I might be interested in, use my card to give me a call." Then he stepped back into the linen closet, closed the door, and was gone with a bang and a bright flash.

The loud sound startled Sabrina out of her daze. "Time? Omigosh, I missed my school bus! I'm going to have to zap out of here!"

A point of her finger scrubbed her instantly clean, but she shivered in her bathrobe. "Those instant showers are *so* cold!" A second finger-wave and her robe transformed into a flashy loose-shirt-over-black-tights outfit. Snapping her fingers twice brought her book bag flying out of her room. As she caught the bag, a final jab conjured up a ring of shimmering light to transport her instantly to the back of the school.

Salem wailed plaintively after her, "What about my breakfast?"

Chapter 2

Salem finally did get his breakfast, although Hilda served it with a heaping side of grumbling. Then she grabbed up her purse and brisked out the door for a shopping trip to Boston, leaving Salem alone to prowl the kitchen for dessert.

Salem believed in dessert after every meal, and he always found it somewhere. In this instance he found the spoon Hilda had used to serve the cat food lying in the sink. After licking it spotless, he rooted through the kitchen trash can and discovered some leftover tuna casserole wrapped in foil. It took his paws a while to get past the foil to the treat his nose detected inside, but he finally tore through and daintily began to munch. The tidbit was a bit old and whiffy by human standards, but Salem's feline taste buds loved it. To hide the fact that he'd been through the garbage again—a strict

10

no-no that usually got him yelled at—he pawed the empty foil into a ball and dumped it back into the trash can.

Now, dozing on the sun porch, Salem was too preoccupied with the glories of digestion to hear the linen closet door open upstairs. It was the clack of unclipped toenails on the kitchen floor that first caught his attention. Then a snuffling sound accompanied by low muttering drifted out from the kitchen.

"He's *gotta* be here! It's logical. Somebody else is obviously paying the rent, and he would never leave a spot so cushy. So he's gotta be here. Question is—is he *home?"*

The voice, although gruff and rasping, was somehow familiar. But nobody else was supposed to be in the Spellman house. "It's that pest Noir," Salem whispered to himself. "Bet he thought nobody'd be home and he could prowl the house undetected. Boy, is *he* gonna get a shock!"

Salem stood up and silently slunk back into the house through the kitty-flap in the French doors. Immediately his nose was assaulted by the reek of cheap cologne. Sure enough, someone was moving behind the kitchen island. Salem leaped up onto the island and shouted, "Caught you, you snoopy dog!"

Then his jaw dropped in shock. Instead of the trenchcoated detective from the Other Realm he expected to see, there, between the island and the stove, stood an enormous sheepdog. "Hey, wait a minute! You *are* a dog!"

The dog was easily five times Salem's size, with a shaggy black-and-white coat that was already shedding on the floor. Sparkling eyes peeped out from under long hairy bangs, and a slobbery pink tongue lolled out the side of his mouth. The pooch turned excited eyes upward, but when he saw the cat gawking down at him, his eyes misted over with confusion.

"Salem?" the dog said in a very canine but clear voice. He glanced to his right, to his left, then up and down. "Salem, where are you? Are you throwing your voice again like the time you made me think that anchovies could talk?" His gaze landed back on the cat, and he pulled a doggy frown. "And when did you get this stupid cat? Salem?"

"I *am* the cat, you dolt," Salem snarled. The horror of recognition crept over him. "Sweet suffering sardines! Gotham . . . ?"

The dog's head slowly tipped to one side, as if he were a puppy confronted by some brand-new phenomenon that he simply couldn't fathom. "Salem? That's you? Gee willikers, when did you become a *cat?*"

"Gotham, when did *you* become a *dog?*" Salem countered.

"I asked first," complained the dog.

Salem fidgeted and turned away. "Drell turned

me into a cat thirty years ago over a small error in judgment," he muttered.

"You mean, your plan for world conquest?" Gotham began pacing excitedly. "Oh, that was so much fun! In fact, it was the most fun I ever had. Considering, of course, that I had never had fun before because I never had any friends before, so it was the only fun I ever had. But even if I *had* had fun before, I'm still sure it would still be the most fun I ever had."

Salem blinked. "Refreshing to see that your mind is still clear as mud, even if you are a dog now," he noted dryly. "Which happened *how*, again?"

"Well, I got to missing all that fun we used to have, seeing as I was having no fun at all because—"

"Can we fast-forward to the *interesting* part of your story, please?"

Gotham sat down with a loud thump. He cocked his head as if to think about it, then nodded agreeably, sending his long bangs flopping up and down over his eyes. "Sure. Whatever you say. There I was, having no fun, and remembering how much fun we used to have . . ."

Salem heaved a sigh and settled down for the long haul.

"And I got to missing you and decided we should have fun together again. So I decided to get you a nice present so we could have all that fun

13

again." Gotham ducked his head down to the floor and came up with a leather slab in his mouth that dangled long leather straps. "I grought you gre Groot!"

An old, long-forgotten headache suddenly clutched Salem's brain. "Gotham, please don't tell me that's what I think it is."

In answer, Gotham rose up on his hind legs and dropped his present on the island at Salem's feet. "Oh, goody! I knew you'd like it if I brought you the Boot."

Salem stared down at the present and, against his own better judgment, asked, "How did you get it?"

"Well, Drell went away for the annual Benevolent Despot's Convention. I forgot about all his traps and curses, but I discovered it didn't matter—he never even locked his door! I just waltzed into his treasury and took it." Gotham's tail wagged in triumph, *thup-thup-thup,* against the cupboards. "You know all those stories about how dangerous it would be to steal something from Drell? The only hazard I found was a booby trap disguised as a display case of colognes. Well, that and the fact that when I left, I was a dog."

Salem's head sank to the polished countertop, and he tried to cover his head with his paws. "You broke into Drell's Treasury and stole the magical talisman that may very well be the foundation of all his power and the reason he's the head of the

Witches' Council? No wonder that twit Pet Noir was here this morning looking for you."

"Pet Noir?" Gotham shook his head vigorously. "I don't think I like him. I think he has something to do with my being a dog."

"Of course he does, you ninny! He's Drell's security agent! He used to be a bloodhound until Drell gave him a human form. He still thinks like a dog, though, so Drell set up a spell to turn burglars into dogs so Noir could track them easier. *Capisce?*" Salem reached out and shoved the Boot over the side of the countertop. It fell, barely missing Gotham's cold, wet nose, and landed at the dog's shaggy feet. "You've got to take this thing back before Drell finds out it's missing," he said flatly.

Gotham, forgetting he was in a dog's body, tried to shrug. Dogs can't shrug, so he almost fell on his face instead. When he recovered, he said, "I don't understand. This is the boot that Alexander the Great wore when he conquered the world! Everybody who's owned it became all-powerful—Julius Caesar, Augustus, Napoleon, Drell—you can use it to take over the world and we can have all that fun again."

"It'll help me get a permanent job as Drell's footstool is what it'll do!" Salem snapped. "Take it back, Gotham."

Both dog and cat froze as they heard the thumping of heavy footsteps upstairs. A husky voice floated down from the landing. "Saberhagen? I've got some more questions for you."

Salem's fur bristled. "Noir's here again! You left the closet door open, didn't you?"

Gotham goggled at Salem in stupid confusion. "What do we do?"

"What do you mean, *we*, dog-breath? I'm innocent!"

The footsteps thumped hollowly down the stairs. "I smell that dog here, cat. I knew you were in this up to your collar. You're both coming back with me to face Drell."

Salem's jaw fell open and then snapped shut. "Well, that answers any questions about just *giving* the Boot back." He whirled around and started to leap off the counter. "Quick—grab it and let's make tracks!"

Salem landed lightly on the linoleum and dashed for the kitty door. Too late, he realized that Gotham's burly sheepdog body would never fit through such a small opening. His claws slipped and slid wildly on the polished floor as he tried to scrabble out of the way in time, but he didn't make it. Seventy-five pounds of hairy dog slammed him nose-first into the French doors.

Gotham's "woof" turned into yelps of pain as Salem squeezed himself free and frantically clawed his way over the dog's back. "This way!" the cat hissed, and sprinted for the hall.

Before he made it a strange *sproing* sound reverberated in the doorway ahead. Salem caught a glance of something small bulging down from the top of the doorframe, and then the whole doorway exploded into silvery filaments that, in seconds, spun and twisted themselves into a huge ropy spiderweb that blocked all passage. With a startled yowl, Salem pulled a tight U-turn, throwing his head and shoulders around until they practically met his rear end still going the other way. He charged back for the kitchen, his rear end sorting itself out and his feet pawing for purchase. He overshot the turn and brushed one of the glowing spiderwebs with the tip of his tail.

The webbing immediately clung to Salem's fur—this was a spiderweb designed to capture *witches!* Like a living thing, it tried to get a better grip on the cat's tail, but Salem clawed at the molding of the wall and hauled himself paw over paw away from the grasping strands. Gathering his hind feet beneath him, he thrust forward with all his might, howling as fur pulled away from his tail, permanently caught in a coil of the imprisoning web. Never mind that—he was free!

Salem broke for the dining room, only half aware of Gotham galloping along behind him. He made it through the dining room into the living room without running into any more surprises. Cautiously he stuck his head around the doorway to peer down the hall from the other end.

As he had figured, he saw the back of Pet Noir's trenchcoat. The canine-turned-human was peeking through the magic spiderweb into the kitchen. All Salem needed to do was pad softly across the narrow hall and silently ascend the stairs. He could be safe under Sabrina's bed before Noir knew he was gone.

Salem hadn't even lifted a paw to move when he heard a heavy *scritching* sound. From the corner of his eye he saw Gotham hurtling at him from the dining room, the Boot's straps looped around his neck, the Boot itself flying around Gotham's head like a satellite. The dog was backpedaling madly, but the polished wood floor kept him skidding directly toward the cat.

Dog collided with cat and both tumbled into the foyer. Pet Noir spun around and made a fast throwing gesture at the animals. He repeated it.

With two soft *splats* a pair of magic spiders landed, one on the living room doorway and the other on the chandelier. Immediately, both began spinning out strands of glowing silk that floated through the air until they touched another surface. Then the spiders scuttled out along the line and with unimaginable speed began spinning huge spiderwebs. As the webs grew, the strands thickened and became ropy. Salem realized that if he didn't right himself and make it up the stairs in about five seconds, the entire foyer would be draped in spiderweb and he'd be caught.

"Icky stickies!" cried Gotham in horror. The threat of danger suddenly filled him with the urge to rescue something, anything. He rolled over and, grasping the scruff of Salem's neck gently but firmly in his jaws, he bounded up the stairs, taking them two steps at a leap.

At the top he slid on the hall carpet and slammed heavily into the far wall, but he used his powerful hind legs to shove himself clear and hurl himself and his burden toward the open linen closet.

Hanging by his scruff, buffeted by the Boot as it jerked around on its straps, and bludgeoned from beneath by Gotham's madly pumping front legs, Salem barely had an idea of what was going on, except that his life was going into the Dumpster and it was all Gotham's fault.

His last memory was of rushing toward the stacked linens. Then there was thunder, a flash . . . . . . then Nothing.

Chapter 3

☆

The school bus dropped Sabrina off at the corner of Collins Road, a half block from home. As she approached the white Victorian house with its squat corner tower she noticed that the front door stood slightly ajar. Was there something wrong at home? She hurried forward.

Reaching the driveway she saw Hilda's car parked alongside the house. Sabrina slowed down. *Maybe Aunt Hilda had her hands full and forgot to close the door,* she thought. It was supposed to be a calming conclusion, but it did little to dispel the growing sense of foreboding that Sabrina felt as she climbed onto the porch.

Gingerly she pushed at the open door and called out, "Aunt Hilda?"

A muffled voice answered from within the house, "Don't come in!"

Sabrina, not recognizing the voice, felt her heart leap. Something was very wrong here. What would be the best thing to do? Run for help or barge straight on in?

Wait—what was the point of running for help? She and her aunts were witches! Anything that could threaten them would be more than a match for mortal authorities, besides being *very* hard to explain. No, Sabrina had to handle this herself.

Summoning up her courage, Sabrina created a magical flash ball and hefted it in her hand. If something was in there menacing her aunt, a sudden blinding light should distract it. She hoped. Feeling as if she were caught in some bizarre scene from a cop drama, Sabrina kicked the door open and threw the ball onto the floor.

The door banged into something before it could swing all the way open, but in the brilliant light of the flash ball Sabrina clearly saw that Aunt Hilda was there and she was alone—but she was hanging motionless in midair, stuck in a monstrous spiderweb!

Then, as if to taunt Sabrina, the door rebounded and slammed closed.

This time Sabrina didn't hesitate. She grabbed the doorknob and boldly shoved the door back open. "Aunt Hilda—"

"Sabrina! Don't touch the webs or you'll get stuck, too!"

"Webs?" Cautiously Sabrina poked her head

inside and looked around. The web that held Aunt Hilda was enormous, stretching from floor to ceiling just beyond the door. More spiderwebs festooned the doorway leading to the living room and hung in lacy sheets from the ceiling of the foyer. Down the hall Sabrina could see even more webs blocking off the kitchen like monster doilies. All the strands shimmered with magical energy like real spiderwebs heavy with early morning dew. They were kind of pretty, but under the circumstances, Sabrina had no time to appreciate their artistic merit.

"What's going on, Aunt Hilda?" Sabrina demanded. "Are you okay? What do I *do?*" She was almost on the edge of hysteria.

"First of all, calm down," said Hilda. "We just have an infestation of Other Realm spiders. They evolved to trap magical creatures and, as you can see, they're really good at it. If you can get into the kitchen we have a can of Web-Away in the secret cupboard."

That sounded simple enough. Sabrina raced around the outside of the house to the sunporch. Cupping her hands against the glass to block the sun's reflection, she peered inside to find the kitchen interior free of webs as far as she could tell. Carefully she entered and made her way to the secret cupboard where the Spellman sisters kept all their witchy household supplies.

Seconds later Sabrina was hurriedly reading the instructions on an aerosol can of Web-Away.

"Could you hurry up?" Hilda called. "I have an itch that's driving me crazy."

"Okay, I think I've got it." Sabrina approached Hilda's web, noticing from this side that it was strong enough to hold her aunt tight without even sagging. Pointing the nozzle at the web's farthest ends, she pressed on the nozzle.

The Web-Away shot out in a thick emerald mist, coating the web strands and making them glow. Then, with a sizzling sound reminiscent of bacon frying in hot grease, the great spiderweb twitched like something alive and lost its grip on the door-frame. The web—and Aunt Hilda—thumped to the floor in a wad, magical sparks skittering up and down each thread. With a puff of green smoke it crumbled to a gummy powder.

Hilda pulled herself free, her clothes stained with the residue of the dissolved strands. "Eww! I *hate* these things," she grumbled, brushing her clothes in annoyance. "The spiders don't attack anything bigger than a fly, but their webs are a *major* pain."

Sabrina gestured at the strands still blocking the living room. "They need webs *that* big to catch flies?"

"These are Other Realm flies, Sabrina," Hilda explained. "They've been known to carry away turkeys."

Sabrina dropped into a combat crouch, pointing the Web-Away defensively. Her eyes, wide in alarm, flicked from room to room. "Where are they? How'd they get in?"

"Probably blew in the last time somebody used the linen closet." Hilda peeled a web strand out of her hair and, flicking it with disgust onto the floor, said, "But you know, I can't remember ever seeing so many of them show up so fast. And now that you mention it, I was hanging there for an hour and a half and I didn't see a single spider anywhere."

That was all Sabrina needed to hear. She maintained her defensive crouch, taking no chances. "Maybe Salem chased them and caught them," she suggested warily.

"That wussy? Hah!" snorted Hilda. "He's deathly afraid of spiders. Probably from that weekend he spent in Drell's dungeons after he was caught trying to take over the world."

"Hey, that's nothing to make fun of," snapped Sabrina. When Hilda looked at her strangely, she added, "I mean, not that I'm afraid of spiders or anything. It's just . . . well, not fair to say bad things about Salem when he's not here to defend himself."

"You can think of a better time?" Hilda shot back.

It took Sabrina and Hilda two hours and another can and a half of Web-Away before the Spellman house was cleared of the last spiderweb. Zelda came home about halfway through the job and followed behind them, magically directing a pair of towels as they scrubbed web dust from the walls and ceilings.

By the time the three witches had finished cleaning up their house and themselves, they were too worn out to cook. They eventually agreed on conjure-in Chinese for dinner. It wasn't until they were sitting down for Szechuan in the dining room that Sabrina realized that Salem hadn't shown up for a while. Quite a while, in fact. *Come to think of it,* she thought, *I haven't seen him since I've come home.*

"Have either of you guys seen Salem around?" she asked, balancing dim sum with a pair of chopsticks.

Zelda spooned hot-and-sour soup into three bowls. "Now that you mention it, no."

Hilda was busy piling her plate high with shrimp in lobster sauce and chao-shu-bai. She paused long enough to say, "I told you, the spiders spooked him. He's probably hiding under your bed."

"He's not. I looked," said Sabrina. Her cheeks reddened. "I mean, not that I was looking under my bed in case there were spiders there or anything. I was just looking. And he wasn't there."

"It's not like Salem to skip a meal," Zelda observed.

"Not that his waistline would notice," said

Hilda. "He's run off before when he was embarrassed about something. He's probably out bullying mortal cats on the fence circuit until he feels superior again."

Sabrina reluctantly decided that her aunt was probably right and dove into dinner. So it was bedtime before she thought about Salem again. Throwing on a jacket and walking around the outside of the house, she called his name. No answer came, no golden eyes appeared out of the darkness. Sabrina screwed up her face in frustration and went back inside.

Her mood wasn't improved when she couldn't find her bathrobe. She spent ten-minutes looking for it everywhere, then finally remembered that she'd transformed it into her school outfit that morning. In an instant she changed it back.

Her hand found an unfamiliar bit of cardboard in the pocket—Pet Noir's business card. It was white with a head-and-shoulders picture of Noir and his name on it, but no telephone number or address. How would someone contact him, then?

With a shrug, Sabrina set the card up against her alarm clock and climbed into bed. The little white rectangle was the last thing she saw as she turned out the lights.

☆

Chapter 4

☆

Salem and Gotham were Nowhere.

Literally.

A vast featureless blank surrounded them on all sides for as far as the eye could see. There was nothing above their heads, nothing under their feet. It had been that way ever since they'd passed through the linen closet.

Despite this total lack of spatial reference, Salem somehow felt like they were moving when they walked, and they'd been walking for . . . what, hours now? Days? Who could tell? But one thing was clear—it was all Gotham's fault.

"How *could* you transport yourself somewhere without having any idea where you were going?" Salem snapped after yet another long, uncomfortable silence.

"I *told* you I was sorry," Gotham whined. "I was too busy *doing* to remember about *thinking.*"

"For nobody else is that an either/or question," the cat sneered.

Gotham hung his head as he galumphed along. "Salem, I couldn't let that horrible man catch us."

"I already told you, he wasn't a man, he was a dog in human form."

"Whatever. He was trying to catch us and take away the Boot I brought you so you could take over the world."

Yes, the Boot. Salem glanced at it hanging around the big sheepdog's neck like some bizarre piece of doggy jewelry, swinging back and forth by its thong and every so often smacking Gotham in the chin. So much trouble for such an unglamorous scrap of leather.

The Boot actually looked like an ancient sandal. Long thongs rose from the top opening, meant to lace firmly up a human leg. Salem knew that back in historical times it had been known as a *caligulus*—a Latin term used to describe the footgear of the average Roman soldier. What made this footgear remarkable was the list of its previous owners.

Beginning with Alexander the Great, the Boot had been worn by some of the world's most powerful leaders. Julius Caesar and Mark Antony had fought over it before Caesar defeated his rival and became dictator of Rome. He had bequeathed it to his adopted heir, Octavius, who became better known as Augustus, the first emperor and founder of the Roman Empire.

From there the Boot was passed on from emperor to emperor as part of the Imperial Treasury. It was taken by Attila the Hun when Rome fell. A Corsican private named Napoleon Bonaparte found it in the Louvre and went on to rule most of Europe as the first French emperor. How Drell got it was still a mystery, but seemingly overnight he sailed to the top of Other Realm politics and took control of the Witches' Council. The Boot had the sweat of world conquest rubbed into its very grain.

Salem had dreamed about the Boot ever since he'd learned of its existence. But since it was locked away in Drell's treasury, surrounded by who knows how many protective spells and fearsome curses, he'd never had the nerve to try to take it.

Now it was here, in his grasp. Could a Salem-dominated world be far off?

Unfortunately, the answer was yes. He was stuck in a cat's body these days, and commanding troops would be hard enough without them sniggering behind his back because he couldn't open his own cans of tuna.

And what troops did he have at his command, anyway? An airheaded former witch who was now a sheepdog—a sheepdog in serious need of a bath—who had managed to bring him the tool for world conquest with the impending wrath of Drell already attached.

As much as he hated the idea of giving up such a powerful talisman, Salem knew he had to get the Boot back to the treasury before Drell returned. The cat's visions of world domination shattered, replaced by a worn slab of leather that swung back and forth in front of him.

Salem suddenly registered that the Boot had been swinging fairly rhythmically before. Now the swing was more of a jerk, and the reason was that Gotham was fidgeting, his hind legs shifting weight from one to another.

"Can we leave now, Salem?" the dog asked plaintively. "I think I need a tree. Or maybe a fire hydrant."

Salem sighed. Leave it to a *dog* to need a tree at a time like this. Then again, they couldn't stay Nowhere forever.

As far as Salem knew, there was only one way out of Nowhere, and it was *not* a route he relished traveling. He stopped walking and primly sat down. "Gotham," he said, "with you around, I can barely smell anything except eau de mutt. However, if you can get that cold wet shiny thing at the end of your face to work, you can sniff out the Line and we'll be able to go—*leave,* I mean. Then after *we* go, *you* can go."

"Oh, that would be good, very, very good!"

Gotham cheered. Then he stopped and looked at Salem blankly. "What's the Line? I know what *a* line is, but you sound like you're talking about a particular one, which is kinda weird, since I don't see any lines anywhere. Actually, I don't see much of anything except nothing."

"Nowhere, not nothing." Salem's exasperation expanded another notch. "Look, it's all explained in the *Handbook*. Just how did you get your Witch's License, anyway?"

Gotham smiled with doggy smugness. "I just kept at it. After the first century, it got easier. Every time I came back, my Quizmaster had fewer and fewer questions for me. I think he wanted me to pass," he confided.

"More likely he just wanted to get rid of you," Salem muttered. Louder he said, "Okay, listen. The *Handbook* chapter on Relative Metaphysical Spatiality defines the Line as the underlying connection between all the parts of the Other Realm. It's the distilled essence of Existence, and it weaves its way in and out of every locale in the Other Realm. If you find it and have the right spells or a travel pass, you can get *from* anywhere *to* anywhere via the Line in seconds."

Gotham gave Salem a big doggy grin, his pink tongue hanging out of the side of his mouth. "Didn't understand a word of it," he said cheerfully.

Salem rubbed his face with a paw. He tried again.

"It's like a subway that goes through all of the places in the Other Realm. You can't see it from the outside, but from the inside it looks like—"

Gotham's brow furrowed with confusion as he interrupted Salem. "You know, since I became a dog, it's hard to remember what things look like."

Salem snorted. "You had a head start on that one. Now that you're an animal, you're going to have to learn to remember what things *smell* like."

Gotham was more than willing. "Really? Gee. So what does the Line smell like?"

Salem wrinkled his nose at the mere thought. How strong ordinary things smelled once he'd become a cat had been hard to adjust to. As for the Line . . . "Well, it's the concentrated essence of everything conceivable, so it smells like everything—*all at once!*"

Gotham's eyes crossed slightly as he tried to imagine it. "I don't know if that would smell good," he said. "I mean, there're a lot of smells that are good, like bananas and waffles and Nature and stuff—but there are a *lot* of smells that are bad, *really* bad, like rotten potatoes you forgot at the back of the cabinet. Or even worse, like—"

Salem cut him off. "You're on the right track."

"All at once? Eww, that would *stiiiiink!*"

"Bingo." Salem batted Gotham's shaggy leg with his paw. "So quit stalling. Turn on the schnozzle and sniff out something that smells like the *worst* mess in creation, and we'll be out of here in no time."

Gotham stepped away from Salem. He shook his shaggy head and flexed his nostrils—the left one first, then the right one. A snort. Two more. Fully loosened up now, the dog raised his nose and snuffled the air with big wheezy whuffing breaths. Then he paused for analysis and, nodding to himself, squinched up his eyes as if in deep concentration and trotted back to Salem, stopping when his nose pressed up against the cat's face.

Salem hopped backward, ears flat. "Hey!" he yelped.

Oblivious, Gotham stretched his neck full length, running his snuffling nose down Salem's body, heading for his tail.

"Hey!" yowled Salem again, this time taking a swipe at the cold, wet smeller.

Gotham seemed to snap out of a trance. "Sorry. I need a standard for comparison."

"Just get on with it," Salem growled.

The sheepdog lurched forward, unsure in all the whiteness where to put his feet. But the odd sense of shifting space felt very much like ordinary walking if he kept his eyes closed and just followed his nose. Salem watched Gotham recede into the whiteness, then scrabbled forward to catch up before the dog disappeared.

A small eternity later, Gotham suddenly leaped

to his left and scratched at nothing. Scratching progressed to mad digging as Salem trotted closer.

The cat's nose ran into the smell like a brick wall. It was so bad that his whiskers wilted and tears ran down his cheeks. It was so bad that his toes curled inward. It was so bad that it made a sewer smell like French perfume by comparison. He gasped and fought for a way of breathing that didn't involve his nose or his taste buds. "Yep . . . that's it," he choked out, sure that his fur would start falling out in big matted hunks at any second.

Gotham was completely unfazed by the stench. "Oh, goody! And on my first try, too. What do we do now?"

Numbness crept over Salem's nose. He slowly regained the use of his tongue. "Sometimes, if you're right on top of it, you can sort of see the Line if you cross your eyes. Anything happen when *you* try that?"

Gotham obediently rolled his eyes inward like oiled marbles. His furry face lit up. "Wow! It looks like a sewer main. Or maybe an earthworm that swallowed every other earthworm until there was no one left except this one earthworm with all the other earthworms inside of it—"

"Please, spare me the similes." Salem pressed his paw up against his nostrils, wishing there was some way he could take his nose off and wrap it safely up until this ordeal was over. Fat chance. "All right, listen carefully. There are pulses that move up and down the Line, going to various places. At least, that's what they feel like from outside. From inside, it's like being in a transparent subway car. If we had a schedule, we'd have a map and a timetable of which pulse goes to which place and where a decent entrance might be. Since we're stuck in Nowhere, we've got to sort of jump onto the Line like hoboes used to jump onto passing railroad cars. If we're lucky, we'll get in and be able to ride the Line to someplace where we can get directions—and some fresh air."

Gotham twitched and looked down between his paws in surprise. "Whoa, I think one just went by! I felt my feet do a weird shift-thing."

"Which way did it go?" Salem asked urgently. "Left to right or right to left?"

"More sorta like from my tail toward my left front paw, about the second or third toe."

"When you feel the next one coming, run ahead of it as fast as you can, then when it lifts you up, sit down and *don't move again!*"

Gotham nodded his understanding, then cocked his head as he shifted from foot to foot to foot to foot. "I can feel it. I can feel it. I can feel it! It's like a rumbling that's getting closer!"

Salem tensed. "When you feel it swell, start running." He crouched, preparing to spring forward.

"It's almost here," Gotham whispered excitedly. "Almost here . . . almost—got it!" He leaped.

Salem leaped after him, landing ahead of a rising vibration that he could now feel under his paws. Even in the whiteness of Nowhere the world seemed to tilt forward, gathering momentum like some invisible wave building to a crest. A point appeared in the nothingness before him, expanding into a disk, then stretching out toward him like a tunnel. There was a brief sensation of being somehow turned inside out, and then the sense of motion reversed itself. Instead of feeling like he was moving forward, Salem now felt like he was on an unmoving surface and the walls of the tunnel were flashing past him. It was like riding a subway train, only the train stayed still while the world zipped by.

"Sit, Gotham, sit!" Salem ordered, using his best "dog command" voice. Whether it was because of the reflexes of the doggy body or the possible miracle that Gotham could remember to do as he was told, Salem's companion dropped immediately to his haunches.

Salem sat down as well, panting heavily. Cats are not built to be marathon runners. Short sprints are their stock in trade. But Salem had been forced to ride the Line the hard way once or twice before, and the short, usually manic run to "jump" aboard seemed to last forever and left him feeling like a wrung-out sponge.

Inside, the Line looked like an infinitely long tunnel stretching far ahead of them and receding far behind. Sections of the tunnel were bathed in different colors and lighting as the Line connected different places in the Other Realm that were normally far apart.

Two seats magically appeared underneath the cat and dog, lifting them up and then moving them along the Line, gaining speed as they went. In seconds, landscapes outside the tunnel of the Line were zipping by, like museum dioramas seen though the window of a car going nine hundred miles an hour. One instant, they were moving through a forest; the next, under water. In rapid succession of eyeblinks they passed a parched yellow desert, a quaint small-town main street, a blizzard-ravaged mountaintop, and the cold, silent void of interstellar space. Everything felt normal to Salem, but outside the Line, day, night, summer, winter, and every kind of weather possible flashed by without any order whatsoever.

It was enough to make a cat's head spin.

Gotham, on the other hand, sat entranced by it all. He kept crossing and uncrossing his eyes as he examined things, completely oblivious to the mishmash details.

Salem got the impression that Gotham was seeing something different when he crossed his eyes, but when the cat tried it, his stomach rebelled. "Keep an eye out for *anything* familiar," gasped Salem, rubbing his eyes with a paw. "We'll use that as a starting point."

Travel through the Line can be quite pleasant, if the proper preparations are made first. But since Salem and Gotham were surfing the Line—the simplest and crudest way of traveling—they were at the mercy of the speed pulse they'd landed in. The outside world flashed by with the speed of a strobe light.

Gotham seemed immune to all the confusion. Like a Zen master, he simply looked at everything at once and therefore, somehow, saw it all. The fact that he didn't understand any of it didn't bother him. "This is so cool, man!" he howled happily. "I love it! It's like you can run around and see everything you could imagine."

Salem winced. "By definition."

"I can see mountains and alleys and oceans and kitchens and a big bright light heading straight for us!"

Salem's whiskers bristled. *"What?"*

"Yeah, that one. The one that's about to hit—"

The world turned white.

Chapter 5

☆

Pet Noir Confidential Journal
The Case of the Wandering Boot

*I prowl the lonesome beat. I smell the under-
side of the city. I hunt rats—the two-legged-
turned-into-four-legged kind. I'm Pet Noir, licensed dog-at-law.*

*The alarm came from Drell's Treasury, sub-
floor two. Popular opinion has it that Drell's
Treasury is mined with cantrips and curses and
cockroaches. Popular opinion is wrong. Only
the cockroach part is true. Drell is so cheap that
his only security is me and a professional
rumor-spreader. It's a dog's life, but I don't let
it bother me.*

*Before I left my office I loaded my right
pocket with spiders—Kamikaze Eight-Eigh-
ties. They're the latest in personnel immobili-
zation technology. Each spider can spin up to
eighty square feet of webbing in six point four*

seconds. They come with ectoplastic strings for reuse. Lots better than the old handheld nets.

I loaded my left pocket with cookie-bones.

If luck was with me, I'd catch the thief before he left Drell's Treasury. But I wasn't worried. Drell's shape-changing spell would automatically turn the crook into a dog even if he escaped. Changing from human to dog doesn't slow you down as much as the other way around. But with my nose, I knew I could track him anywhere.

When I got to the scene of the crime, the first thing that hit me was a wall of odor—colognes, all of them cheap. The display case of Drell's collectible aftershave bottles had been knocked over and several of the containers had broken, including the limited-edition Elvis one. It was a clever attempt to cover the trail, but I've got the best sense of smell in the Other Realm. I mentally subtracted the smells until all that was left was the scent of the intruder.

I recognized him as a small-time malcontent named Gotham, a schmoe who'd gotten caught up in one of those pyramid empire schemes. The only thing on his rap sheet was aiding and abetting global conquest, sentence suspended in exchange for a certain list of pizza parlors. Why would a no-account like that steal something from Drell's Treasury?

I found the answer when I checked the inventory. The Boot *was missing.*

I thought about that aiding and abetting charge. Maybe someone clever enough to mask his trail with cheap cologne was also clever enough to plan world conquest and make someone else take the fall if it failed. It was a mystery I could sink my teeth into.

My next step was to start checking out my target's likely safe houses. Gotham had been a known accomplice of Salem Saberhagen; Drell had sentenced Saberhagen to a century as a cat, in custody of some Spellman sisters. I looked up their address and stepped through my portal. An instant later and I was at the Spellmans'.

The Spellmans' portal was done up as a linen closet. Good-quality sheets and towels, but too much fabric softener. No trace of Gotham's scent, though. I knocked on the door.

The door opened to reveal an angel in a fuzzy blue robe with white stars. A sleepy and ticked-off angel, but heavenly nonetheless.

The cat was there, just as lippy as I remembered him. He denied any contact and told me his parole officer would back him up. I took him at his word for the moment but made a mental note to check the alibi at the first opportunity.

Before I left I gave the angel my card. Told her to call if there was anything she could do to help me.

I left.

I was on the trail.

Chapter 6

The flash of white became clouds, and the clouds parted to reveal a horizon dividing sky from land—land that was rushing up to meet the two animals at an alarming rate.

With cat reflexes, Salem spun his body around to land feet first on top of an enormous pile of trash. With dog reflexes, Gotham twisted, frantically pawed at thin air, and landed tail first on top of Salem. The two of them slipped from the rubbishy peak and tumbled down the slope into a garbage gully. An avalanche followed them down and buried them in debris.

Salem scrabbled through a sea of junk to the surface. There was nothing dank or rotted about the junk. It was all quite dry and lifeless, in fact. Most of the debris seemed to be scraps of paper—notepaper, calendar sheets, letters, contracts—

none of it whole and all of it scattered to the four winds.

Salem gasped as he surfaced. A rainbow of confetti burst from his fur as he shook himself, eager to loosen the clumps of paper dust that wanted to wedge themselves into his thick undercoat. As far as he could see in any direction, giant hills of trash covered the rubbish plain without a break.

Salem realized that the clumsy sheepdog was nowhere to be seen. "Gotham?" Salem called. *"Gotham?"*

A low hill directly in front of Salem exploded, hurling colorful scrap paper up in all directions. The cloud of debris thinned out to reveal a grinning sheepdog. "Hot ziggety, that was fun!" he barked in joy. "I knew that I'd have fun if I got back together with you, Salem. Let's do it again!"

"Even if we wanted to do it again, which I do not, we couldn't. This is the End of the Line, Gotham—we rode it the wrong way."

Gotham's grin didn't budge, though his eyes glazed over a little. "Huh?"

Salem curled his lip in irritation. "Lost stuff sometimes falls into the Line. Anything loose gets swept along until it gets dumped here. This is where everything broken winds up. Every scrap here represents a broken date, missed appointment, or shattered dream. It'd be enough to make me sentimental if I weren't a cat," he remarked.

44

A thick leather ring binder a yard to Salem's left caught his eye. The binder lay on its back, rings sprung open like clutching fingers. Memos, diagrams, and heavily annotated maps spilled out, to be caught up by the winds and blown about in aimless spirals. Those maps seemed familiar. . . .

A yowl of heartbreak burst from Salem's throat. "My plans!" he wailed. "All my wonderful plans!"

Gotham had started to snuffle through the piles, stopping every so often to dig energetically. At Salem's cry he bounded over to see what was the matter. "Whadja find, huh? Whadja find?" He nosed the binder. "Mmmm, smells like pizza."

"That's all it meant to you, didn't it? Pizza," groused Salem. He stretched out a paw to caress the creases of a map. "These are . . . *were* . . . my plans for world domination. My grand scheme to become the greatest beloved despot in world history. Junk now." He sobbed, a brief, heartrending sound. "Nothing but junk."

Gotham wasn't listening. To Salem all these piles of "junk" represented broken dreams, but to the sheepdog it meant fun. He returned to his cavorting, running up one side of a pile and butt-sledding down the other, over and over. For a real treat, he burrowed down until he was completely covered and then surged upward like a breaching whale, shaking his whole body and throwing debris everywhere.

Salem quietly continued to paw through the

yellowed pages filled with his lost ambitions. "Imagine what it would have been like if I'd had the Boot back then," he whispered. "Think of the troops I'd have commanded. People would be spending money with my picture on it today." He glanced over at Gotham, who still wore the Boot round his neck like some kind of bizarre doggy necklace. "But, *no,* what do I have instead? One lousy follower who couldn't care less where in the world he was, so long as he was happy."

A torn envelope spun in on a breeze and bounced off Salem's nose. He swatted angrily at the paper, ripping it open and scattering its contents. Salem caught a brief glimpse of an ornate card reading, "Happy 500th Anniversary," above a jagged tear. But it was the two stiff strips of bright orange paper that got him excited.

"We're saved!" he shouted. "Saved, I tell you!"

Gotham rolled sideways down a hill of paper to land in a sprawl near Salem. "That's great news!" he barked. Then a frown creased his hairy face. "Saved from what? Were we in trouble?"

Salem patted the slightly torn cardboard rectangles. "These are unused Line passes," he said. "They'll take us somewhere on the Line! Wherever it is, there'll probably be a tourist kiosk that we can get directions from!"

Salem squinted at the tiny printing on the passes. "They were going to Poughkeepsie. Imagine there being a place called Poughkeepsie. And for a second honeymoon, no less. No wonder they broke up instead. Not our problem, though. Our problem is finding a way back onto the Line."

Gotham leaped and pranced around Salem like a hyperactive puppy. "You want to get on the Line, Salem? Is that what you want to do? The Line that smells real bad?"

Salem spat out the tickets. "Yes, yes, and yes."

"Well, a place that *smells* like that other place that we found when we were in that other empty place is right over that hill," Gotham offered, twitching his right ear to indicate which direction he meant.

"Are you telling me you've already *found* the Line?" Salem asked in disbelief. "Here, in all this garbage?"

"Uhhh . . . yup!"

Salem grinned, a rather frightening expression to behold on a feline face. "Gadzooks, what a nose! You've found our way home, pal! Now lead me to it and I'll show you the experience of a lifetime— these are first-class passes." He carefully pinched the passes in his jaws. "Wead de way!"

Gotham bounded up and over a trash dune with Salem hot on his heels. The dog's nose quivered as it sampled the air, and behind his shaggy bangs his eyes crossed from time to time, trying to pinpoint the long Line worming through the mountainous mess around him. Then a unique stench slammed up against his nostrils, like a rotten brick floating in a breeze—that was it! With a happy yip, Gotham made a beeline for a shallow basin up ahead.

Salem was breathing hard by the time he reached the depression in the debris. He caught a good, deep lungful of Line stench and coughed, spitting the passes out. "Oh, yeah, this is it, all right." He peered down at the printing on the passes, now slightly smudged with cat spit. "Let's just hope that the passes still work. Normally you travel by—"

"Clicking your heels three times and saying, 'There's no place like home'?"

Salem hissed at the interruption. "No! You consult a schedule and a map first. Then you command the passes to send you to 1297 sub B 23, or wherever it is you want to go. The Line opens nice as you please, you get on, you ride, it stops, you get off. Easy as kitten chow. But these things"—and he pawed their passes—"are first-class reserved, like for a prepackaged tour. They're activated by a personalized invocation code, which it says here is—"

Gotham beat him to it. "'No matter where you go, I'll be right there by your side'!"

Salem looked like he'd bitten a lemon as he quickly reread the invocation code. "Is that an expression of devotion or designed to scare me?" he muttered. Either way, Gotham hadn't been kidding. That really was the code. With the utter loathing only a cat can muster, Salem said caustically, "And to think I have to say this to *you*. Well, I may have to say it, but I don't have to mean it." His tail twitching with annoyance, Salem placed his right paw on one of the passes and told Gotham to do the same with his. Then in unison, they spoke the invocation code: " 'No matter where you go, I'll be right there by your side'!"

A silvery door appeared in the air before them. With a musical chime, it slid open. The brightness of the sky at the End of the Line prevented Salem from seeing in, so he hesitated. "Let me check it out first, and then follow me in," he cautioned Gotham.

The dog bowled the cat over as he leaped eagerly through the opening without waiting.

Salem moaned, picking himself up. "Okay," he said, *"you* go first and *I'll* follow."

As soon as Salem carried the passes through the threshold and into the Line itself, the door slid closed. The inside of the Line appeared completely different from the last time they'd traveled it. Thanks to the first-class passes, the space that they found themselves in looked like a small but luxurious train compartment. Plush seats sat on swivels so travelers could look out the wraparound windows and see the vistas as they passed by. As soon as Salem and Gotham were perched on the seats, they felt themselves moving forward along the tunnel of the Line.

Gotham nosed one of the windows open and inhaled deeply as the scenery moved past. "This is the life," he yipped. "I could do this forever!"

"I, for one, wouldn't miss you for a moment," Salem said, snuggling into the leather seat. "After we return the Boot and get the heat off my tail."

Unlike their previous trip down the Line, their speed this time was much slower, almost dawdling. The End of the Line slowly slipped away behind them, replaced by a view of interstellar space. Space then gave way to green rolling hills and industriously tilled fields. A farmstead dissolved into a garden patch before being replaced in turn with an aerial view of a plantation. Every place they passed seemed to have some sort of farm or garden in it. Salem batted the passes in annoyance. "We luck out finding these and what do they end up to be? First-class passes for a crawl through Hicksville."

Gotham wasn't complaining. He greeted every new vista with the same slack-jawed, slobbering delight as the Line gently wove its way through pockets of reality, sometimes at ground level, sometimes below it, and sometimes piercing barn walls or haystacks, the objects turning transparent as Salem and Gotham traveled straight through them.

Salem lost count after the 637th farm scene, and, bored to tears, he decided to put himself into a trance. It was either that or go stark raving mad by the time they reached Poughkeepsie, wherever that was. So, with his eyes closed and his meditative cat mind contemplating the wonder of his own heart-beat, Salem was taken completely by surprise when the Line car suddenly dissolved out from under him.

☆

Chapter 7

☆

Sabrina riffled absently through the encyclopedia volume on the desk before her. Her foot tapped out a monotonous *click-click-click-click* on the floor, earning her a stern "Shush!" from the librarian.

"What is *with* you today?" asked Valerie, seated opposite Sabrina. "Is it something I did? I mean, you didn't have to spoil a perfectly good Saturday morning by coming here to study with me. Even though it *was* your suggestion."

Sabrina twisted her mouth and gave her girl-friend a sideways glance. No matter what problems anybody in the world had, Valerie always presumed she was at fault. "I guess I'm just worried about my cat. He didn't come home last night and he missed breakfast this morning."

"That sounds wonderful," Valerie said dreamily.

"What?"

"Oh, not the cat being missing part," Valerie explained quickly, "just the idea of having a pet to miss if it's gone. I've never had one. My mother refuses to have an animal in the house. I bought a cardboard cutout of a dog once. I called him Card. But somehow, our relationship wasn't as rewarding as the ones other people have with their pets."

This was more than Sabrina wanted to know about Valerie's home life, so she excused herself and went down to the stacks—officially to find a book, but in reality just to brood.

The open book stacks of the Westbridge Library consisted of tall steel shelves lined up as closely as possible in the building's deep brick basement. The dim lighting would have made the place seem cold and unfriendly, but thankfully somebody had lobbied to have carpeting put in, so the atmosphere was cozier than one would expect after descending such bleak concrete stairs.

Nobody was rummaging around at the moment, so the very air in the basement hung motionless, waiting for a disturbance, any disturbance to break the tomblike silence. Sabrina's entrance sent a barely perceptible ripple through the room, and when she started pacing, the air molecules themselves might have been bouncing with joy.

Sabrina herself, however, felt anything but joyful. Salem just never missed a meal. For that matter, Salem rarely missed a between-meal snack or a dropped crumb. For him to miss dinner *and* breakfast was a Code Red alert. But what could have happened? Why hadn't he left a note, or at least a clue as to where he'd gone?

Sabrina's fingers brushed against a piece of cardboard in her pocket. It was the card that the funny detective guy had given her. She'd put it on her nightstand before going to bed but had no memory of having picked it up again this morning.

As she'd noticed the previous day, the card bore only Pet Noir's name and a color picture of him. No other information, no contact number, no address, no description of his business was offered. *I guess if you know who he is, you know how to contact him,* she thought, tilting the card to the light to see the portrait better.

It seemed to be a holographic print, because the background moved behind Noir's hat when Sabrina moved the card. In fact, she could see other parts of the room behind Noir if she flexed the card right. She got caught up in trying to see as much of the holographic room beyond the frame as possible, flexing the card this way and that, searching for better angles.

On the third flex, sparks flew from the picture and the image of Pet Noir turned to look out at her. The room behind him had changed into a shabby office. The card itself now felt slightly warm. "Sorry, it's the secretary's year off. Whaddaya need?" Noir said clearly.

"Oh, it's *you!*" Sabrina blurted in surprise.

"Of course it's me, doll. Who'dja expect to get with my card? Lassie?"

Normally Sabrina wouldn't be so rude, but the detective's poor manners made her snap back, "What is it that you do, exactly?"

Noir fixed her with a flat, disbelieving eye. "I'm a shamus, a hound, a tracker. If it runs away, I chase it."

"So . . . you find things, then."

"Not 'things,' sweetheart." Noir leaned in closer until his photo became an extreme close-up. The quirk at the side of his mouth couldn't be called a smile, but it wasn't quite a frown, either. With one finger he pushed his tan fedora hat back just a little, revealing a high forehead and the hint of a hairline, the brown hair slicked straight back. "I'm whatcha might call a specialist," he said in a low tone, almost like Clint Eastwood. "I only find animals. Call it a personal quirk."

"Oh, good! Then I need you to find my cat. He's been missing since yesterday. He's black and his name is—"

"Salem Saberhagen," Noir finished for her. "Already on his trail. He's got a three-oh-two charge—Accessory to Grand Theft Thaumaturgical—hanging over his head. But when I find him, it's Drell I'll be handing him over to, not you. No offense, doll, but Drell holds my leash."

In crisp bites, Noir gave Sabrina a summary of

the Stolen Boot Case. He described the chase through the Spellman house and the escape of the cat and dog.

"So that's where those giant spider webs came from," Sabrina said. "Don't ever let my Aunt Hilda know that or she'll change you into something uncomfortable."

"Been there, done that."

"Yeah, so I see. Okay, look, Pet—"

"Call me Noir."

"Right. Look, Salem wasn't involved. You said it yourself: that Gotham guy stole the Shoe before he came to see Salem."

Noir shook his head. "Boot, not Shoe—"

"Salem's reformed," Sabrina insisted. "He's left his old life behind him like . . . like . . . old litter. The only ambition he has nowadays is to get a satellite dish to watch the Swimsuit Channel."

Noir put a hand over his mouth as if to hide a grin of amusement. Then Sabrina realized that he'd tucked a little wedge of chew bone against his cheek. "I'll give you this," he said thoughtfully. "Each crime has its own scent, as if the criminal has to leave his personal mark. And this caper has a smell all its own—more dog than cat."

"Then you'll let me know if you find Salem? Before you tell Drell?" Sabrina got a little desperate. "Whatever your rate is, I'll pay you—"

"Your money's no good with me."

"You don't want Mortal Realm money? No sweat, I'll get witch money, whatever denominations you want—"

Noir flapped his hand for her to stop. "You're a nice kid, so I'll cut you a break and send you copies of my report."

Sabrina paused, eyeing the detective's bland expression on the little card. "Wait a minute—you're stalling, aren't you? What you're really saying is that you can't find them, can you? Of all the—"

"Sabrina!" came Valerie's voice suddenly. "Hey, did you get lost down here? Are you avoiding me?"

Sabrina immediately stopped talking. After only a few seconds her silence broke the communication spell and Pet Noir's image reverted to its original photo, except that it still retained a slightly 3-D effect. The odd warmth that the calling card had developed slowly faded.

Valerie stomped down the basement stairs and approached Sabrina. "I heard voices. Who were you talking to?" She glanced around. "I don't see anybody else here. Did they leave? Is it my fault?"

Sabrina casually waved Pet Noir's card at Valerie, then stuffed it back into her pocket. "I was just using a, uh . . . a calling card. Latest technology." She brushed past her friend and rushed toward the staircase. "Valerie, I'm sorry but I've gotta go. I have to run home and look up something in a book." She bolted up the stairs.

Valerie frowned after her. "A calling card," she pouted. "Is *everyone* cooler than me?"

As soon as she cleared the back corner of the library, Sabrina zapped herself back into her bedroom. There, lying open on the ornate wooden stand by her bed, was *The Discovery of Magic,* a great leather-bound volume that contained the entire wealth of witch magic.

Hastily Sabrina flipped to the index, running her finger down the topics until she came to Portals: Operation, Maintenance & Upgrades. "Illustration 25.4.95.12," she mumbled as she thumbed to the proper page.

Illustration 25.4.95.12 proved to be a half-page advertisement for the Portico Telegate Company. A two-dimensional block print morphed up off the page to become a small 3-D classical porch done in veined marble. As Sabrina stared at the stone doorway, it magically rushed at her, either growing in size or making her shrink, she couldn't tell which. But an instant later she was zooming past the pillars and in through two great open bronze double doors.

Once past the doors she came to an unsteady halt in a large foyer of classical Greek design. The floor under her feet was composed of vast mosaic portrayals of exotic Other Realm vacation spots. More destinations were depicted in richly detailed frescoes running around three walls of the room—the splendor of the Infinity Falls Hotel, the rustic Nemo's-in-the-Volcano Resort, the very chic Hex Appeal Vacation Mall, and the cult-music mecca Fall from Graceland—four of the Other Realm's most chic getaways.

An alcove set in the far wall facing the door contained several reclining couches surrounding a sunken fish pool. Glittering goldfish roiled the surface of the pool as they swam to and fro, eternally searching for food. A statue resembling the Venus de Milo, only *with* its arms, stood like a sentinel at one side of the alcove.

Attracted by the colorful fish, Sabrina stepped closer to the alcove. The moment she did, the Venus statue moved, stiffly turning her head to beam a perfect smile at the teenage witch. Her pale lips parted and she said with a soft rasp, "Welcome to Portico, the finest providers of inter-Realm transport systems. With Portico, the universe is right outside your door. Please be seated and wait for the next available help-maiden. We apologize for any delay. Infinity is rather large. In order to serve you better, portions of your conversation may be recorded. Say nice things about Drell." With this said, the Venus statue froze once more.

The goldfish tracked Sabrina as she skirted the pool to sit on the farthest couch. No sooner was she settled than the air above the fish pool flickered and transformed into a column of raining gold flakes. The flakes swirled and hovered over the water, causing the hungry fish to leap up and snap at them. They snapped in vain, for everything was a magically projected illusion.

The golden veil drew apart like shower curtains to reveal a dark beauty robed in ancient Greek linens and silks. Her black hair curled into tiny oiled ringlets around an olive face. A thick scroll with ivory handles appeared in her marble-smooth hands. Stepping down to the ground, she gracefully draped herself on the couch next to Sabrina and smiled wide enough to show her teeth, all of them gleaming and perfect.

"Lovely, wasn't it?" she said musically as she gestured to the column still sparkling above the koi. "That's our patented Shower of Gold effect. Welcome to Portico, dear. I'm Calliope. How may we help you?"

Sabrina wasn't sure just how to proceed. She wanted to find out how to track Salem, but she didn't want to bring a lot of attention to the cat, just in case Drell got wind of it. She tried the direct approach. "I need to know how the portals work."

Calliope's face turned stony. "I'm sorry, that's a trade secret," she said primly. "Will there be anything else?"

Sabrina's heart fluttered in her throat. Her whole plan hinged on finding out how to track Salem. If she couldn't do that, then Drell might wind up with brand-new catgut strings for his violin! If the direct approach wouldn't work, maybe an appeal to scholarship might.

"I, uh, have to do a report on them for my Witch's License," Sabrina bluffed. "Just the general mechanisms, you know, how they get you somewhere, how you might trace somebody's trips—"

Now Calliope's demeanor turned positively frosty. "I'm sorry. That involves privileged information. A portal trace can only be authorized by the Witches' Council or by Drell himself. I can't discuss it further." She sniffed, obviously disapproving of Sabrina's line of questioning. She began to rise. "I'm sorry we can't help you."

Sabrina resorted to the pathetic approach. Actually she wasn't faking it. At this point she really felt desperate! "Look, you've gotta help me," she said, her expression crumpling into a portrait of worried frustration. "I'm only a novice witch and my cat is missing. Nobody's seen him since he went through our closet and I think he's in terrible trouble."

Calliope listened with interest, then with alarm, her stony demeanor softening to sympathetic butter. She dropped her formal facade and squealed in a matronly voice, "Here, now! Why didn't you tell me that to start with? I've never had a cat, but I have had a few gargoyles in my time." She gazed into the distance as if in fond remembrance. "Such cuddlesome beasts—and cuter drain spouts you'll never see. Takes the loneliness out of a hard day on the pedestal." She focused back on Sabrina. "I'm always willing to give a young witch a broom up the ladder of learning. What do you need to know, dearie?"

"How does a portal get you from place to place? No—I mean, how does it know to get you where you want to go?"

"Well, our patented Aur-O-Meter spellware does a complete ectoplasmic analysis of the traveler's chakras," recited Calliope, "to determine how best to transport the traveler—living up to our Realm-famous claim of ninety-nine percent successful transportations. Not one fatality this year, if you don't count that little incident out on Pluto. He may be frozen, but he's still alive. Technically."

Sabrina looked confused, so Calliope simplified her explanation. "Basically, we read the traveler's mind. One should always have a clear idea of where one wants to go before stepping into a portal. The spellware picks up the mental image and sends the traveler there."

"Can you track where somebody has gone?"

"The built-in spellware is designed to create an ongoing traffic log. If you show an image of the traveler to the log, it will tell you where they went on their most recent trip. Records older than that aren't accessible without permission from the portal's legal owners."

As Sabrina digested this, Calliope slipped back into her professional persona. "Now, honey, would you be interested in one of our upgrade packages? We can equip your . . . just a moment, I'll look up what you're currently operating. . . ." Calliope unrolled her scroll, and the parchment whizzed from one roll over to the other as fast as a microfiche. "Ah, here we are. You've got a linen closet, I see—a Suburban Queen model, isn't it? Well, we can provide you with the *cutest* transport effects for your closet traveling. Our specials include Celestial Elevator, Digital Dissolve, and the ever-popular Puff of Smoke. There's no extra charge for installation and, of course, it's instantaneous—"

But Sabrina was already zooming out of the *Magic Book.* She had a plan to pursue.

Chapter 8

Salem stalked down the red dirt road, his tail twitching with annoyance. A few paces behind him, Gotham trotted along. Since the dog's legs were so much longer than the cat's, Gotham had to weave back and forth across the road in order to stay behind. This wasn't as much of a problem as it seemed, because Gotham found so many things at the side of the road to sniff that he was forever having to sprint to keep up.

The road cut across gentle rolling hills that were almost too green to believe. It ran up slopes, past small clumps of trees, and down into rich dells, each with its own little stream at the bottom.

Gotham finished his examination of a small maple and raced up to Salem's side. "I'm sorry, Salem," he said earnestly for about the fiftieth time. "I don't know what got into me."

64

"I don't hear you," sneered the cat. "I refuse to acknowledge the existence of someone who would get us—I mean, *me*—dumped off the Line and into this . . . this . . . 4-H heaven. I've seen enough cattle and compost heaps to last the rest of my nine lives."

"But I said I was sorry."

"Why do dogs *have* to stick their heads out of something that moves? You broke the spell that ran the first-class passes!"

"I was just trying to smell all that neat stuff that was going by. I didn't know it could break."

"That's another thing," complained Salem. "If *I* tried that excuse, everyone would say that I should have known better. How does being clumsy and stupid make a dog . . . yuck . . . *lovable?*" He switched his tail in irritation and stalked down the road.

Cresting a hill, Salem gazed below them at yet another tidy little farm. Like the dozen or so they'd already checked out, he figured this one would have a surplus of offensive odors from nameless sources, but not that distinctive stench that would identify it as a gateway back onto the Line.

A long fieldstone sheep wall ran beside the road up to the gate. The whitewashed gate itself bore a sign proclaiming the place to be HOGG FARM. Salem slunk under the lowest board in the gate, bending in impossible places so that no whitewash from the wood touched his fur. Gotham took the fence with a leap that peaked too soon. The top rail hit his belly and pushed the breath out of him. He teetered back and forth for an instant, then scrabbled his way over the fence, leaving deep claw scratches in the paint.

From their hiding place in a fencepost, three tiny mice scampered out to watch the dog land inside the yard, narrowly missing the cat. In unison they shrilled in high-pitched voices, *"The faaaaarm has viiiisitors!"* Then they giggled so hard they nearly fell off the rail.

The farm consisted of a house and a barn, with a few scattered sheds. A rickety brick tower sat like a rocket at the back corner of the house, its many openings allowing pigeons to enter the coops inside. The birds reminded Salem that he was hungry.

At first glance the enormous barn looked like a giant haystack. Closer examination revealed that the "stack" was in fact a sturdy thatched roof that rose from low stone walls to a roof ridge that rivaled the house's brick tower in height. Chickens and ducks milled about in front of the barn doors. They also reminded Salem that he was hungry.

A herd of woolly sheep wandered in the field beyond the wall. Lambs frisked in the sunshine while their mothers chomped tall, sweet grass. Salem was about to scream from the tranquil serenity of it all when an old ewe raised her head her sensitive nostrils identifying the whiff of strangers in the air.

Before she could panic, Salem jumped up on the flat stones of the wall and addressed the ewe. "Uh, hi there. We're new in the neighborhood. Anybody here who can give us some directions? Or something to eat?"

"Me, too," whuffed Gotham, stretching up to peer over the wall.

At the sight of the dog, all the little lambs bolted from their play and hid behind the flock. The old ewe began bleating, "Wooolf! Wooolf! He'll biiite us! He'll eeeeat us!" The others joined her cry, making a terrible racket.

"Hey!" said Salem. "I'm not *that* hungry yet. I'd settle for some table scraps—you know, leftover pot roast, macaroni and cheese crusts—even that tough skin you cut off ham."

"You got a taste for ham, cat?" boomed a grumbly bass voice behind Salem. The cat and his dog companion whirled around to face the biggest pig Salem had ever seen. The pig stood five feet high at the shoulder and was nearly nine feet long. He weighed easily a ton, and though he had no tusks, he had the rest of his teeth and sharp little trotters to boot. Even though Salem was sitting on a wall, the boar was so tall that he had to look *down* his callused nose at the cat.

Involuntarily, Salem's back arched and his fur bristled at the boar's cold stare. He calculated the odds of his being able to dodge a pig at this distance and groaned at the unpleasant answer.

Gotham, however, wasn't fazed in the least. He wagged his tail like a propeller, jumping and cavorting around the massive porker. "Hi! Howarya? I'm Gotham and this is my pal Salem and we're lost. What's your name?"

The boar swung its head ponderously toward the dog. This was obviously not what he had expected as a response from trespassers. He grunted an answer. "Bubba."

"Oh, that's a good name," Gotham said enthusiastically. He sat down and cocked his head to chew the taste of it. "Punchy, short, to the point. A little southern, maybe. Not that I have anything against the South. I've never been there, myself. It's just to the right of the East, isn't it? Or is it the other way around?"

Salem had to wrench the conversation back from the brink of blather. He smoothed his fur and sat down at polite attention. "I'm sorry of we got off on the wrong paw, sir," he told the pig slowly and carefully. "I won't talk about food if you won't stomp me into a grease spot. We just want to ask for help getting back on the Line."

The huge head pivoted back to the cat. Tiny eyes peered out from behind rings of fatty flesh. The long, almost feminine lashes didn't blink. Then, flatly, "Never travel. That's for humans."

"We don't mind," said Salem, donning his best

used-car salesman smile. "Some of my best friends are human."

"And I used to be," woofed Gotham. "But now I'm a sheepdog."

Wariness came back into the boar's eyes. "No vacancies," he grunted at Gotham. *"I'm* the sheepdog around here."

Gotham was all sympathy and commiseration. "Oh, were you human once, too? That's bad. That's even worse than being a dog."

The beady eyes glittered dangerously. "I've always been a pig. What's wrong with being a pig?"

Salem tried desperately to avoid disaster. "Nothing, nothing at all," he said quickly. "On you it looks good."

The three mice on the railing shrilled, *"The piiiig thinks he's a sheeeepdog! Heeheeheehee!"*

Salem glared at them, flexing on the wall.

"Ignore them," Bubba advised him. "We do." His touchiness shifted again, forgotten for the moment, and he set out to clarify things for Gotham. "I'm not actually a sheep*dog,* I'm a sheep *pig."* He fixed Gotham with his eyes, daring contradiction.

Salem decided that further conversation could only prove dangerous. His eyes widened in kitten-like sincerity. "I assure you that neither Gotham nor myself has any ambitions in animal care. All we want to do is find a way onto the Line and beat it back home."

Every other farm resident they'd stopped had greeted that request with a look of distrust or accusations of rude fixations. Bubba didn't flinch in the least. "That'll be the bog. I suppose I could let you sniff it, if I went along with you. Actually, it's one of my favorite spots. At my size, the usual mud wallow only mucks my knees."

The pig walked over to a sheep gate in the wall and nosed the latch open. He indicated for Salem and Gotham to follow.

Moving faster than he expected, Salem followed the giant hog across the field. For a two-thousand-pound beast, Bubba moved quickly on his tiny feet. The field soon ended at the crest of a hill overlooking a wooded hollow.

Bubba's path wound downhill around several stands of birch and dogwood, and the air acquired a sharp stench. As the land to either side of the path became soggier, frogs and newts skittered among the rotting leaves, stirring up noxious fumes.

"It's enough to make a cat lose his lunch," complained Salem. "If he'd had one. . . ."

Bubba was far ahead of them now, oblivious to their bickering, but he wasn't hard to find. A ton of hog is hardly the most silent of beasts. Bubba's width exceeded his length and anything under a foot in diameter didn't stand a chance against him. Bushes crunched beneath his feet and saplings crackled like dry spaghetti. All the animals within hearing wisely fled the area.

The path began cutting through real swampland. Salem leaped from rock to root, trying vainly to keep out of the muck. On a particularly tight turn through a stand of mangroves, Bubba rounded a massive tree and disappeared suddenly from view. A hideous *shlurk*ing sound froze Salem and Gotham in their tracks.

Silence greeted them when they crept around the turn. Salem cringed at the sight before him. Like an Olympic-size pool of slime, an evil-looking expanse of syrupy water filled a clearing in the swamp. Lily pads that seemed to glow with pale rotting light bobbed as ripples raced across the pond.

The immense hog was nowhere to be seen.

"Bubba fell into the lake!" Gotham barked. "Quick, Salem! We have to save him!"

"It's a sewer, not a lake," said Salem, "and if Bubba's fate depends on my going in . . . in . . . *that*, then he's doomed to be mud-pickled porker."

A vile, gigantic bubble burst upward from the pond, ejecting an enormous splatter of goo. The stench was unbearable. Streams of brackish water and muddy slime drained away from the bubble, revealing a huge hog shape that glared down at Salem with beady little eyes. "That'll do, cat," Bubba warned.

"This what you were sniffing for?" demanded Bubba.

Gotham inhaled the moist heavy air with gusto.

"Whuf!" he sneezed. "That's ripe, all right. But the Line's not here."

"What?" Salem gagged. "You sure it's not here? It's *got* to be here. Where else could smell worse?"

Gotham shrugged. "Sorry, Salem. We're still lost."

Chapter 9

☆

Sabrina sat on her bed and flexed Pet Noir's card three times. The picture sparked from photo to person and turned to face her. "You again?" barked Noir. He had a certain weatherbeaten charm, but his social skills definitely needed polishing.

Sabrina reminded herself that Salem's fate depended on her keeping a level head, no matter how hardheaded Noir might act. "Have you found any trace of them?" she asked.

Noir's snarl of frustration was as clear an answer as if he'd shouted, "No!"

"Well," said Sabrina. *"I* know how to find out where Salem went through the linen closet."

Noir gave her an aw-shucks tug of his hat brim. "Great, doll. When this is all over, I'll see to it that Drell sends you a little something, by way of thanks."

Sabrina waggled a finger at the once-dog detective. "Uh-uh-uh, you don't get it that easy. I'll take my reward in advance, thanks. Two things." She held up one finger. "One—let me come along with you to look for Salem. And two—promise to let me prove his innocence before you take him to Drell."

Noir peered out from under his hat brim and grinned wryly. "Nice try, doll, but it won't wash. I'm the lone-wolf type, see? When I walk down a street I like to hear the echo of my own footsteps. Solitude is my only companion. Besides, I'm a professional. This is no job for a kid."

"Like you're not right out of high school yourself," Sabrina commented archly.

Noir looked offended. "I'm three," he growled.

"Three." Sabrina's eyebrows rose to her hairline. "Three . . . ?"

Noir blushed. "Sorry. I keep forgetting I have to multiply by seven. I'm twenty-one." He shrugged himself to his full height and added proudly, "But I'm the best tracker in both Realms. I'm the top tail."

Noir's boastfulness irritated Sabrina as much as Libby Chessler's smug superiority. She couldn't resist the temptation to needle the detective. "And what happens if you *don't* get the Boot back?"

To Sabrina's surprise, Noir grew thoughtful and then shivered inside his trenchcoat. "I'd say that Drell would be very unhappy with me. Worse, though, *I'll* be unhappy with me. I've never lost a quarry. I got 'em all, every one." He grew thoughtful again and, jamming his hand into his pocket, rummaged around, produced a small rawhide chewie, and popped it into his mouth. He worked his jaw, staring into space. "I don't think I'd be able to curl up and sleep at night if I ever missed one. I'd tail that pigeon until I brought it down or broke my heart trying."

Sabrina baited the hook. "So you'd do anything you had to in order to keep your record?"

"It's not the record, it's the principle. But, yes, of course I would."

"Then you *have* to let me come along!" Sabrina insisted. Before Noir could protest, she raced through her argument. "Point to you—you have no idea where Salem and this dog guy went to when they ran through the linen closet. Point to me—I have a way of finding out. Point to you—you want to catch your burglar and stay top dog in your field. Point to me—I want to prove that Salem didn't do it. Point to me—you *admitted* that the dog guy actually stole the whozis. Point to me—I'd come along whether you wanted me to or not. See? I have more points than you. Set, game, and match. I'm going."

Noir looked like his chewie had gone bad. He scowled and snuffled in frustration. "Hmph. You got me by the choke chain, doll."

"Whatever," said Sabrina. "Let's get going."

Noir snapped his fingers three times. His image

turned back into a photograph and he himself appeared in Sabrina's bedroom. His nostrils flared as he looked around. "Nice place, even though it reeks of cat."

Dubiously, Sabrina took a sniff. "I don't smell anything except my cross-trainers."

"Human noses!" scoffed Noir. "If you're lucky, you can smell your upper lips. My nose can tell if a cat's been in a room in the last six weeks and what it ate for dinner before showing up. My nose is legal evidence, doll."

Sabrina held up a long black whisker. "Good. Then you can swear that this came from Salem, right?"

Noir's nose twitched ever so slightly. "ID'd," he agreed.

Sabrina glanced down at the open pages of *The Discovery of Magic* to fix the proper spell in her mind. Dropping the whisker, she flicked a finger at it. The whisker dissolved into multicolored neon glitter.

The glitter swarmed in the air like bees for an instant before shifting and crystallizing into a 3-D diagram of a cat. The schematic essence of the image filled out, fuzzing and sharpening in detail. A moment later, a slightly transparent copy of Salem hung in midair.

And then dropped to the floor like a sack of flour.

The substitute Salem landed on his feet in the best cat tradition and glared silently up at Sabrina, just like the original would have. The girl shrugged and smiled apologetically. "Sorry."

Sabrina led Noir and the Salem simulacrum to the linen closet door. The door opened, but the Spellman linens were no longer to be seen. Instead, the door faced a marble counter topping four columns.

"Portico Portal Service Counter, how can we serve you?" A speaker grille set in the center of the counter squawked.

"I'm a licensed operator of this portal and I'd like to see the Travel Log, please," Sabrina said.

The counter vanished and a stocky tree-person appeared in its place. Thick evergreen needles bushed from the top like hair. A stubby stick jutted from the upper part of the trunk, just below two deep-set knots. Below the stick, a deep slash of a mouth cut across the bark, exposing the wood underneath. Leaning its knobby wooden elbows on the counter, it regarded Sabrina with two knot-eyes. "What can I do for you?" Its voice was as polite and gentle as a summer breeze.

Sabrina scooped up her Salem duplicate and placed it on the marble counter. "Calliope said you could tell us where this traveler, er, cat went on his last trip. Can you do that?"

The Travel Log glared at her then, dropping its jaw to display the fine-grained rings of its interior. "See these, Missy? What do you think they're for? Each and every ring is a complete trip record. How else do you think I got this job?" It snorted in disgust. "Can I do it. . . . Function follows form, you know."

A ring of twisted light appeared above the substitute cat. With a strange buzzing sound it began to spin, going faster and faster until it became a blur. Then it settled down over the simulacrum, its buzzing sound softening to an analytical purr. Layer by layer the substance of Salem's double dissolved and was sucked up by the spinning ring until all that was left of the cat image was a single black whisker lying on cold marble.

The sampling done, the spinning ring of light disappeared. The Travel Log bent its attention inward, apparently consulting its rings. "This traveler went Nowhere," the Log finally announced. "Regulations allow you to retrace this trip one and one time only."

The linen closet door slowly began to close. The Log faded, its breezy voice blowing one last time out of the vanishing service counter. "This fulfills your maximum allowable information. Thank you for choosing Portico. Have a nice trip."

Sabrina blinked at the closed closet door, stunned. "Nowhere? *That* was an answer?"

Beside her, Noir showed no sign of confusion. "Nowhere," he breathed. "What an unexpected choice. It's positively brilliant!"

"This means something to you?"

Noir didn't hear her. In fact, Sabrina didn't seem

to exist to him at the moment. "Nobody goes Nowhere," he muttered in fascination. "It's almost impossible to reach. Archmages and senior wizards train for decades to achieve the Zenlike ability to blank their thoughts enough to visualize infinite Nothing! But under hot pursuit, that dog did it in an instant! What a brain!"

He began listing options and building a plan. "The only way to get out of Nowhere is to jump the Line. Not a problem, though. I have a Line hook. I can jump the Line, hook in, and invoke manual override. I can troll for traces of Line hopping and I can cast Line alerts down the Line to other agencies."

"I should have made you promise to explain things to me, as well," Sabrina complained. "What does all this mean?"

"It means, change your clothes, doll," Noir said, his eyes alight with the thrill of the hunt. "We're heading Nowhere, fast."

Chapter 10

Pet Noir Confidential Journal
The Case of the Wandering Boot

We—I've never had to put a "we" in this journal before—we picked up the scent where the targets had jumped the Line out of Nowhere. Without the angel's help, I might never have tracked them.

At the End of the Line, all the evidence showed that the dog was looking for something. The cat just sat in one place, but the dog was definitely searching for something. I had to figure out what that was.

And then it hit me—

"Ouch!"

Sabrina picked up the cardboard slips that had fallen from the sky onto Pet Noir's head. A lot of things had been raining in from everywhere—or, more accurately, from Nowhere—while Noir had walked around the dump speaking into his portable recorder. "You always have to talk like that?" she asked him.

He snapped his recorder off. "Doll, I work the gutters on the graveyard shift of Life. I've trotted from uptown to across the tracks, through alleys and through parks. I know every lamppost and fire hydrant by name. I run with the common pack. I sing the song of the streets, and I'm not ashamed of my breed."

Sabrina gave him a blank stare.

"Sorry," Noir said. "But you can't graduate from Detective School until you learn how to talk like that and keep a journal of cases."

"O . . . kay," Sabrina said slowly, handing him the cardboards and walking away. "You win, here's your prize."

She hadn't gone three steps when a spatter of confetti showered down on her. Noir had told her to change her clothes, but she'd been too distracted to listen. Now she could see the reason for his advice. She zapped herself a long tan trenchcoat and fedora, much like Noir's, and ambled over to the trashed ring binder that Noir had already pinpointed as the place where Salem had been sitting. She poked idly at the sheets of cramped, dense writing. Clipped to the back of one cover were photos of plastic troops in various positions on a world-conquest game board called Threat.

Her heart skipped a beat as she recognized them.

"Noir! These are Salem's old plans for world conquest! This proves that he's innocent!"

Noir trotted over. "How so?"

"Well, if Salem really wanted the Boot to take over the world, he'd have recovered all his old plans, too, wouldn't he? He didn't, so he's innocent."

"I'd already figured that out, doll. You know, for an amateur, you make a pretty good detective. But you've got a long way to go to catch up to me." With a flourish he held up the pasteboards that Sabrina had handed him. "You let *this* vital clue slip right through your fingers."

Sabrina glanced at the pasteboards. "Those look like concert tickets."

"They're a pair of Line passes with the scent of your kitty and his pal all over them. This was their escape hatch from here. Obviously, this is what the dog was looking for." Noir stuffed the passes into his pocket. "Clever," he mused. "Very, very clever. But they made a fatal error, as all criminals finally do. They left their passes inside the Line—which means that *they fell out* of the Line—without ever making the full trip to Poughkeepsie."

"What's obvious to *me* is that you've been watching too many private-eye movies," said Sabrina. "If you've got a lead, can we just get out of here? This place gives me the creeps. Besides, I want something to eat."

Noir pulled a cookie-bone from a pocket and offered it to Sabrina. She was amused by the gesture but declined the treat. "I'd rather have something from a kitchen, thanks."

Noir shrugged and put the treat back in his pocket with one hand while his other hand pulled a TV-remote-sized Line detector from the other pocket. As he had back in Nowhere, he waved the device around until the needle in the display swung into the red zone, indicating that it had detected the nearest intersection of the Line.

Assured that he had a valid response, Noir pushed the detector's "Go Online" feature. Two magical hooks shot out of a tiny recess in the detector's case and raced to lodge themselves into the invisible substance of the Line. For a moment, the hooks tugged at empty air before opening up a door. Noir repocketed the Line detector and motioned for Sabrina to follow.

Since Noir's Line detector was a no-frills utility device, there were no plush seats inside the Line. Instead, two loops of leather like subway straps hung from the nonceiling for them to hang on to as they moved down the Line. To Sabrina, it felt like some bizarre theme park ride, with locales whizzing by like animated dioramas—or maybe a typical music video edited into shots the length of an average eye blink. Since Noir knew exactly where they were going, their trip made no allowances for sightseeing. Just as Sabrina got used to the flash-by scenery, it was time to go. They stopped and she followed Noir out onto a small patio.

Leafy shade trees sheltered the tables and chairs set on the patio, creating a cozy and comfortable dining spot, but Noir ignored the outside seating and ducked into the building itself. He led Sabrina through a small but bustling restaurant kitchen whose workers smiled at her as she passed.

The dining area beyond the kitchen was not much bigger than the Spellman living room, but Sabrina somehow felt immediately at ease there. A handful of booths ran alongside a U-shaped counter whose scarred top and worn stools declared a place dedicated to comfort over fashion. A plate-glass window faced a quiet little suburban sun-drenched street that could have been anywhere in America. Filling up most of the window, however, was the name of the restaurant. Sabrina decoded the backward lettering: THE BIG KITCHEN. "Wow," she said to Noir. "You really took me literally."

"Best eatery in both Realms, in my opinion," Noir replied. "Grab a stool at the counter."

As soon as they sat down, a well-worn coffee cup appeared on the counter in front of Noir and an equally inelegant glass appeared before Sabrina. She took an experimental sip from her glass and her eyes popped open in pleasant surprise. "What is this? It tastes . . . heavenly."

"Of course it does. It's ambrosia fizz," said a new voice in the room. "Imported directly from Olympus."

A woman in an apron glided in from the back room. She looked to be in her middle years, but her smile radiated a youth and energy that Sabrina seldom saw in her schoolmates. As impossible as it seemed, the smile got wider as the woman said, "Hi, welcome to the Big Kitchen. I'm Judy the Beauty on Duty."

Noir frowned at Judy over his cup. "Don't you ever serve coffee here?"

"Of course we do." Judy smiled affably. "To anybody who needs it. But you need rabbit bouillon more."

"You never give *anybody* what they want. It's amazing that you get any repeat business."

"That's because we do better—we give people what they *need.*" Judy turned to examine Sabrina critically. "You look like you've got an active afternoon ahead of you, so instead of that burger you're thinking of, try a Southern Rush." A generous plateful of food appeared in her hand. "Six different kinds of fruit in yogurt for energy and a sprinkling of dark chocolate morsels for that vital sugar rush."

Sabrina was skeptical, but she tasted the dish anyway. An electric tingle rushed from her taste buds to her fingertips. Her fork was in her hand and the plate on the counter before she realized that Judy had retreated to the kitchen, beaming like a Buddha.

Halfway through her meal Sabrina noticed Noir sitting next to her nursing his full cup. "Bunny bouillon not agreeing with you?" she asked.

"Nah, Judy's right, as usual. It's just what I need to calm me down. Problem is that she serves it in a bottomless cup, so it always looks like I've never touched it. You can turn that into a metaphor if you work on it. Makes me think."

Noir returned to his introspection. Sabrina decided it was time for her to move things along. "Hi," she said. "I'm Sabrina Spellman, I'm half witch and half mortal and I'm studying for my Witch's License."

Noir blinked in surprise. "What was all that about?"

"I just told you about me. Now it's your turn to tell me about you."

"Why would you want to know about me?"

"It's called conversation. I hear that it's the latest fad. You should try it."

Noir shrugged. "Well, my lineage is hardly anything to wag a tail about. I'm a mixed breed," he confessed, though with an undertone of defiance. He took a long sip of his bouillon before continuing. "I come from way up north. My pop was a werewolf and my mother was an icicle sprite—second cousin to Jack Frost himself, she was. She melted soon after I was born.

"Dad did what he could for him and me. He taught me to hunt and to track. Many's the full moon I remember loping at his heels, chasing anything that moved. I'd inherited his skin-changing ability, and he insisted that I not neglect my human half. I went to school as often as I could, but since I aged seven times faster than a human, it seemed like I was moved into a new grade every month."

Here Noir paused. He took a long drink of rabbit bouillon before continuing. "It was just after my first birthday. I was looking forward to graduating from high school. And then Pop, who was hunting in the mountains, got snatched away by a giant roc.

"I dropped everything and set out to track that bird. I followed it across the Other Realm, following a trail that was seldom more than droppings, lost feathers, or the occasional village stomped flat. I tracked it to its lair in the heart of the Neverglades and, in my human form, trapped it and dragged it to Drell for justice.

"Drell sentenced the roc to spend a hundred years as his pet parrot, living in a redwood behind his palace. If people really tick him off, he makes them clean up under the tree. He seemed impressed with my skills and offered me a job as his security chief—but I had to choose to be either human or wolf to qualify for benefits. Different packages, you know. With Pop gone, there didn't seem to be much reason for staying four-legged. I made my choice, and now there's nothing I can do about it." He drained his cup and sat brooding silently.

"Guarding Drell's Treasury is a walk in the park," he said after a moment. "It's security, but I'm a rover at heart. I yearn for the thrill of the chase, the rich smell of frightened perp ahead, the all-or-nothing contest of me versus the prey. It's the only thing that makes me feel alive anymore. That's where that dog of your cat's comes in. The more I think about it, the more that dog seems to be at the center of all this. He's an enigma. Everyone I've talked to thinks he doesn't have two brain cells to rub together. No one believes he could possibly be intelligent. It's genius, I tell you! It's the perfect cover. He's a challenge I can't resist."

He turned to look Sabrina in the eye. "Okay, doll. You got your deal. You prove the cat didn't do it and he's free. But the dog is mine, see?" He offered his hand.

Sabrina took it and shook firmly. "You're sort of okay—for a tortured soul who's trapped in the wrong body." She remembered the spell of hers that had misfired and caused her boyfriend, Harvey Kinkle, to switch bodies with a dog. *Harvey,* she thought, sighing. He was a million miles and another Realm away from her.

Maybe Noir detected how much she missed her friend. He smiled back at her as he held her hand. "You know, this companion thing isn't too bad. Makes me want to wag my tail." His face twisted in sudden pain. "My tail! My poor lost tail."

He let go of Sabrina's hand and crumpled to the counter in grief.

Chapter 11

The road ended abruptly at the edge of a bizarre forest. Huge grotesque trees like redwoods crossbred with mangroves filled the valley from horizon to horizon. The trunks of the trees ranged from forty to a hundred feet in height—but all those trunks began at least fifteen feet above the ground. Instead of being sunk into the earth, the roots of the trees curved in great loops and hoops between their start at the trunks and their deeper parts burrowing underground. The trees did indeed look like they were walking, or at least standing, on tiptoe. Passage through the forest was impossible except where the roots aligned to make an arch-covered path.

Salem and Gotham had been walking on the largest and most well-trodden of these paths for a long time.

"Have I told you how much I *hate* this?" demanded Salem.

"Yeah," Gotham replied cheerfully. "Constantly."

While Salem pouted, Gotham continued. "I always wanted to travel around and see as much of the world as I could. That's why I went into pizza delivery—it took me places I'd never been before."

"That explains why you were always lost."

"I always thought that helping you take over the world would be heaps of fun and I'd get to see a lot of it while we conquered it. It was pretty boring without you, Salem. That's why I decided to bring you the Boot—so I could get to see new stuff."

"Nice to know that my doom would provide some novelty in your life."

"But now that I've seen the Line, I think I could spend my life in there." Gotham spoke in a dreamy voice. "In fact, I see it every time I close my eyes—and sometimes when they're open, too. It looks—"

"Look here—see how there's been more traffic down that path than any of the others? That's obviously the main drag. That's where we go."

Gotham vigorously shook his head no. "Salem, I think we're supposed to go down that itty-bitty path over there."

Salem gave an imperious sniff. "You're a dog, what do you know? But I'm a cat—top of the food chain."

"How can you say that? People are top of the dogpile. They domesticated the animals."

"Show me what domestication gets you," Salem sneered. "In exchange for food, shelter, affection, and not ever enough belly rubs, you dogs have given up your self-respect, your dignity, and the ability to resist howling when a siren goes by."

"Sounds like a great deal to me!" said Gotham, feeling all frisky at the very thought of such a life.

"Cats, however," continued Salem, "have taken that same deal and turned it on its head. We never come when we're called. We sit on the person most likely to be bothered by it. And if anything goes against our dignity, even by a hair, we counterattack with a good snubbing. People do whatever we want them to. Sounds like the definition of domestication to me."

Gotham didn't quite follow what Salem was talking about, but it sounded so confident and leaderly that he felt his doggy heart pledge eternal loyalty. As he had done when they'd both had their normal witch bodies, Gotham vowed to follow Salem and protect him always, wrong or right. So when Salem trotted, Gotham was right behind him.

The dog didn't give another thought to his own choice of path. That memory had already dissolved back into the fluid of his mind. Besides, there were more than enough strange new things to see and smell. And the world looked so wonderfully *different* when he crossed his eyes now.

The timeless atmosphere of a land without sky led Salem to quickly lose all awareness of how long they had walked or how far they had gone. But his stomach lived by its own clock, and the alarms were ringing. He was *hungry*.

No sooner had he become aware of how famished he felt than they came upon an offshoot path, running at right angles to the one they were on. EDIBLES THIS WAY an arrow-shaped sign declared. The offshoot path was clearer of weeds than the main way. It looked like there had been a lot of traffic turning off to find out just *what* was edible.

"I believe this is our turn," Salem announced, and trotted onto the crosspath.

Gotham fidgeted uneasily. He'd just renewed his pledge to follow Salem come what may, and already that pledge was being tested. "I'm not so sure, Salem," he whined. "Something about this doesn't smell right. I sense undertones of deception and suppressed malice, all mixed in with anxiety about eating."

Salem actually laughed. "Sounds like a typical roadside café to me!"

"I dunno. It smells dangerous. I'd turn back if I was us."

"This brilliant scent analysis brought to us by the fellow who's been a dog such a short time. Gotham, lad, do you remember our little deal about decision making?"

"Uh, yeah, but—"

"No buts about it. I need nourishment. I'm a cat. If I don't eat at least five times a day I get cranky. And you reeeeally don't want to be around when I'm cranky."

A vague whiff of something wonderful drifted out at them from the bypath, a mere thread of delicious aroma, undefined but somehow promising undreamed delights to the palate, if they would just trace the smell to its source.

All debate between Salem and Gotham evaporated. A glaze settled over their eyes and saliva pooled under their tongues. In rapt silence they trotted slowly up the path.

The narrow track led straight as an arrow through the root loops of the trees until it came to a small clearing and a shabby lunch stand, its urban decay contrasting harshly with the intense forest surrounding it.

The stand was little more than a long box set behind a lunch counter. A half-circle awning, its fringe wind-ripped to jagged pennants, hung over cockeyed stools listing their separate ways. By way of a dining patio, a semicircle of pink flagstone matching the awning in size stretched forward from the counter.

Salem leaped up onto the countertop to look around, while Gotham contented himself with putting his paws up on the counter and stretching his full length to peer around. Running along the rear wall was a fine collection of food preparation equipment, but nothing seemed to be actually cooking. The tantalizing smell wasn't coming from anything already prepared. There was no sign of a cook or waiter, although a large chalkboard menu on the back wall bore a message saying, YOU NAME IT, WE'LL SERVE IT.

"Ooh, a self-serve café. I love it," said Gotham. "If I could have it, I'd have a big bowl of chili. I haven't had really good chili in a long time."

"That's your idea of proper food? Even for a dog you have no taste," criticized Salem. "If I could have anything I wanted, I'd order a double tuna casserole or a seafood splendor selection."

In a snap the aroma coming from the lunch stand abruptly changed. Instead of just smelling like *something* delicious, the aroma definitely smelled like chili and fresh-cooked fish. And where there had been nothing on the countertop, now there were two large bowls and a platter. The bowl in front of Gotham held steaming beans covered with a spicy meat sauce so rich it was nearly black. From a yard away, Salem's eyes winced at the intense chili smell. His suffering didn't last long, however, because the bowl in front of his place held a crunchy combination of baked fish and macaroni, while the platter was heaped with more ocean produce than a sushi bar. The chalkboard on the wall now read, EAT UP!

"Hot diggety," woofed Gotham. "Let's eat!"

"Not so fast," interrupted Salem. "Sure, it's a

good offer. But I'm not taking a bite until I know what it's going to cost me."

The blackboard squeaked briefly and changed its message. NOT A CENT. THINK OF IT AS A POOR ATTEMPT TO END HUNGER IN THE FOREST.

"I can live with that," said Salem. "I'm all for charity, as long as I don't have to contribute." He took a careful taste of the casserole. "Mmm. Nice and crunchy, the way I like it."

Gotham had already inhaled half of his chili. He stopped to judge the taste. "You know," he said, orange grease staining his lower jaw, "I can never get chili hot enough. I'd love some extra-dextra super-duper hot sauce to put on this."

The words weren't even out of his mouth when a large bottle filled with red liquid appeared on the counter beyond his bowl. Gotham squinted at it and complained. "Oh, more than that."

In a twinkling, the entire back edge of the counter filled full-length with an army of hot sauce bottles, their peppery contents perfuming the air from their open tops and bringing tears to Salem's eyes. Gotham was stunned. "That'll be enough, I guess." He reached out a paw to lift up the nearest bottle, but it slipped from his claws and toppled over, spilling sauce all over the counter.

Salem did a double-take. Maybe it was his imagination, but he could have sworn that the old counter surface sizzled where the red juice stained it. But it wasn't sizzling now.

Gotham was terribly embarrassed. "Forgot I don't have hands anymore. Guess I'll just settle for the chili."

For a few moments the only sound in the clearing was the slurp of happy tongues lapping. Gotham finished his bowl of chili in an instant and was overjoyed when it immediately refilled itself. "Ooo, it's even got spaghetti in it this time!" He began slurping anew.

Salem, ever the dainty eater, munched one delicacy at a time, moving back and forth between the casserole and the seafood platter. Time seemed to slow as he savored the finely sliced tidbits of lobster, shrimp, and scallops, his whiskers quivering at the luscious taste of it all.

He wasn't even half-full when he realized that time wasn't really sluggish—*he* was sluggish. An odd feeling of fatigue was creeping over him like a warm blanket. Sure, he got sleepy after a good meal, but usually he didn't fall into a digestive coma until after he'd eaten his fill. And oddly enough, it was getting dark all of a sudden. With effort, Salem lifted his head from his feast and peered out of the shack.

Something was wrong.

Beyond the awning of the snack shack the silvery green light of the forest was dimming. The ragged edges of the awning were stretching downward and firming up, becoming sharper and thicker, more like sharks' teeth than canvas shreds. Likewise, the pink flagstones marking the edge of the patio had turned their broken edges upward and were also changing into a serrated line. And was the ceiling actually coming down at him?

Salem's mind slogged along at the speed of cold maple syrup, but a single urgency drove him to move—he *had* to get out of there, *now*. Sleepy thickness made putting one foot in front of another a hopeless task, leaving him to lurch across the counter, tumbling one open bottle of hot sauce after another into the throatlike void growing at the back of the shack.

The back wall rippled and dissolved into a bottomless tube lined with pulsing red folds that made an ominous sucking noise. As the opening of the shack narrowed to less than a yard across, the counter, the stools, and even the floor itself tilted backward toward the *shlurk*ing throat.

Panic gave strength to Salem's legs. Desperate to flee but almost completely robbed of his sense of direction, he scrabbled along the length of the counter, toppling all the hot sauce bottles and sending Gotham's bottomless chili bowl crashing to the flagstones.

His food suddenly gone, Gotham looked around himself for the first time since starting to eat. He opened his mouth to object to Salem's clumsiness but got only a glimpse of the cat and the great gullet behind him before the predatory shack reacted to the first of many pints of ultra-hot sauce tumbling down into the depths of its stomach.

The snack shop twitched in unexpected agony, its outward facade quivering, its rigid walls and floor flexing like rubber. Restaurant fixtures lost their texture and became red fleshy protrusions that writhed from pink walls. A deep rumbling made the place shake, frightening Gotham and activating his dazed doggy instincts. His chili-drenched jaws closed on Salem's midsection in a rescue reflex just as the rubbery shop convulsed and spit them both violently down the path. The jagged edges of the awning and the patio, now completely transformed into teeth, snagged hunks of woolly dog pelt as Gotham's body scrambled away.

Gotham got one glimpse of the chalkboard, which now read, ow, ow, ow, ow! before he slammed into a tree root and darkness claimed him.

Chapter 12

☆

Pet Noir Confidential Journal
The Case of the Wandering Boot

I hadn't meant to spill my guts to the angel.
She just seemed so . . . sympathetic. Maybe
that's the real reason all the great detectives
work alone. I locked my feelings back in their
kennel and struggled to get my mind back on
the case.

Never mind what Drell thought about Saber-
hagen, I was now convinced that the dog was
the brains behind the whole thing and the cat
no longer mattered at all.

"Excuse me?" Sabrina interrupted Noir's pocket
dictation. "What do you mean, 'no longer matters'?
I don't know this Gotham from Adam. I'm here to
rescue Salem. Will you put the recorder away and
talk to me? Noir? *Noir?*"

We left the Big Kitchen and got back on the Line. By doubling back toward the End of the Line, it was a snap to pick up the fugitives' scent and follow it to find the general area where they'd left the Line. That was a new puzzle—I couldn't for the life of me figure out why they'd chosen that place to bail out. That area was the most rural section of the Other Realm. Since the introduction of malls and conjure-in fast food, most witches had moved upRealm, leaving the place and the animals there to run wild. Once again, my two-legged form would set me apart from a place where I would otherwise have fit right in. I felt a sharp sense of pain—

"Ow!" Noir barked, jolted out of his narration as Sabrina punched his arm again.

"Don't you *dare* ignore me!" Sabrina repeated heatedly. "You may think that dictation routine is cool, but you come across as lame RetroTechno Streetnik." She mimed checking a dipstick. "Your reservoir of human interaction is a quart short."

Noir was tired of losing his private space to a partner, even if she was an angel. "Can't you see I'm tired of human interaction?" he snapped. "All humans do—mortals and witches alike—is lie, cheat, steal, and forget to put dinner out on time. Just once, I'd like to know what my life would be like if I'd chosen the other way. The way of four feet and a tail. Where the other dogs I ran after were pals and not perps."

Sabrina's patience had worn thin as well. "Are you going to dream of puppyhood all your life?" she snapped. "Even if you were still canine, you'd probably have litters or grandlitters by now. Six or eight sharp little mouths chewing on your ears would have you screaming to have your human form back, pronto. Look, until last year, *I* didn't know I was a witch. In that time I think I've made every mistake in the book—and they *gave* me a magic book to keep track of them in. Not to mention a *Handbook* and a 'Cut that nap short, Sabrina! It's testin' time!' Quizmaster. Life is tough all over."

Noir blinked in confusion, unable or unwilling to grasp Sabrina's message.

"Okay, let me translate it into private-eye jargon for you," she said. "In the game of life, you play the hand you're dealt. Barring more magic, you're a people now, not a dog. Play or fold. Are you ready to fold because you think you have the wrong number of legs, Noir? Well, are you?"

Noir stared at the recorder in his hand. His thumb itched to press the REC button.

Sabrina barreled on. "Besides, stereotyping is no justification for a career. You don't have to be somebody's watchdog all your life." She flung her arms wide, proclaiming, "Live life without a choke chain!"

Noir wilted. He reluctantly slipped the recorder back into his pocket. "Actually, nobody's ever listened to any of my case records, not even me."

"If you want to talk," Sabrina said, "try explaining to me in simple English what you're doing."

Noir opened his mouth to object, then closed it again. Taking a slow breath, he held up the Line passes. "We're here because you found these. They should have taken your friend and his dog to their printed destination. For some reason, though, Salem and Gotham left the Line about here and dropped the passes as they left."

"Then all we have to do is follow them through that farmland until we find them, right?" said Sabrina, pointing at the greenery outside the Line. "Should be a snap for the King of the Noses."

Noir looked stung. "I guess I deserve that for bragging so much. There's a hitch, though." He gestured at the Line around them. "In order to connect every place in the Other Realm at once, the Line sort of has to fudge on time. We can jump out here to follow the perp—er, Gotham and your friend Salem—but *we* might arrive before *they've* gotten there."

"Say *what?*"

"It's too hard to explain. Just believe me when I tell you that time in here is not the same as time out there."

Sabrina tried to imagine time as being some kind of fluid that could move in waves. Oddly enough, she could almost feel a sort of vibration under her palms and soles. The vibration increased sharply in pitch.

Noir must have felt it, too, because his head jerked from side to side as if trying to locate the source of the feeling. He grew alarmed as the interior of the Line began to ripple like moving water. He threw himself on top of Sabrina, shouting, "Incoming! Get down!"

No sooner had he spoken than the very air rang like a bell. A spot on the wall bulged inward as a shaggy figure appeared out of nowhere. Noir was astounded. "It's the dog!" he shouted.

It *was* Gotham, but there was something transparent about the sheepdog, and he seemed to be aiming himself at something that neither Sabrina nor Noir could see. He also seemed to be riding an equally invisible wave that carried him away down the Line until he vanished beyond sight. In seconds, the only trace of his passage was a shimmer in the air that pulsed like a fading echo.

"Mangy phase-shifter!" Noir cursed. "I would have caught him, but he was traveling a minute ahead of us."

"You mean . . ." Sabrina gasped in amazement. "You mean we just saw him run by in the *future?*"

"Approximately," Noir answered. "I told you time works differently here. And that dog seems to be able to come and go at will. He's a born Line-surfer. He can make the Line take him anywhere he wants. He could be anywhere by now." Noir stared down the Line, admiration filling his face.

"You can start a fan club later," Sabrina said crossly. "If Gotham just went—or *will have gone*—thataway, how are we going to find out where Salem is right *now?* He's the one I want to rescue, remember?"

Before Noir could answer, the Line rang like a bell again, and Gotham appeared in front of them. *"There* you are! I *knew* I'd find you somewhere in here because I knew you were following me, but I forgot that you'd be following me *ahead* of me."

Noir pulled out his Line detector, pointing it at the sheepdog and shooting golden energy hooks into the dog's coat. "You're under arrest for Grand Theft Thaumaturgical," he barked. "Come along quietly!"

Gotham ignored the hooks. "Unh-unh," he woofed. *"You're* the ones who have to come along. Pigs! They've got Salem! They've got the Boot! Big dogs—alpha males! I can't fight them! You've got to rescue him!"

He spun around and vanished through the wall in a single leap. Noir frowned and twiddled the controls of his Line detector.

"Follow him!" shouted Sabrina, covering her ears as the air rang again.

"Relax," said Noir. "I've got him hooked. It'll take a minute or two to get a fix and then we'll be on his tail like fleas."

Sabrina forced herself to wait. "What was all that about pigs and dogs?" she asked. "And what's an alpha?"

Noir intently scanned one wall of the Line with his detector, moving forward an inch at a time. Without taking his eyes off the display he explained, "An alpha is a dominant male. Usually bigger than the others. Could make a simp like Gotham grovel in an eyeblink. It's how rank works in the dog world. My pop was an alpha. He was tougher than anyone in the North." Pain crept into Noir's voice. "If I had my original shape, maybe I'd be an alpha, too. But I'm just a puny two-legger. We're in for trouble."

Sabrina flexed her index finger. "Salem's in danger," she said dangerously. *"You* just find him and let *me* take care of the trouble."

☆

Chapter 13

☆

Salem and Gotham silently agreed that a short rest was in order. Escaping from an ambush by a carnivorous fast-food stand took a lot out of one. Gotham nosed out a cave in the tangled roots bordering the path and they squeezed in. Salem even ignored his slime-streaked fur and collapsed next to the dog.

Though the shack had been a magical illusion, the food it had served had been solid enough and still spattered the cat. But it didn't smell like fish anymore.

Gotham leaned over and began licking off the goo.

"Hey! Don't eat that," Salem protested. "You don't know what it is—was—might have been."

"It's not bad," Gotham said between slurps. "Tastes like mushrooms." He paused, his eyebrows creasing in confusion. "Funny . . . for a while I coulda sworn it was chili." He went back to licking.

"Let's hear it for the Fleabag Gourmet," said Salem, trying to wriggle away. Gotham pinned him to the ground with a paw. "What are you *doing?*"

The dog blinked in surprise. "I owe you. You saved my life from that . . . that *thing.*"

"Yeah, well, it was an accident." Salem stopped wriggling. "Anyway, that *thing* was a Hunting Lodge. They dig in near roads and highways and lure victims in by overriding their brains with hunger-inducing vapors. This was a young one. Mature ones lay out entire buffets to swallow whole tour groups."

Gotham curled his tongue around Salem's tail and licked a last smear from the tip. "You don't understand," he said. "What happened proves that I was right. You *do* like me."

Gotham stopped licking and stared at Salem with big wet puppy eyes. "I once heard you tell Hilda that as soon as your world takeover was complete you were going to give me the Boot," Gotham said shyly. His half-hidden eyes brimmed with tears. "Imagine being entrusted with something *that* important. That meant you liked me— really, *really* liked me."

Salem looked away. When he said give Gotham the boot, he hadn't been talking about the powerful Boot, but rather getting rid of Gotham. "Yeah. Well. Let's talk about it after a nap." He snuggled up against the warmth of the dog's belly. His head rested on the scuffed leather of the Boot. "Say good night, Gotham," he muttered.

"Good night," Gotham replied. A second later the dog asked, "Or did you mean you wanted me to say good night, *Gotham?* That would be strange, because I should be saying good night, *Salem.* But if you wanted me to say it another way, I would, of course, even if it didn't seem to make sense, like that time you . . ."

Salem let Gotham's ramblings lull him to sleep. Perhaps it was the faint aura of power clinging to the Boot, but he dreamed that he slept on a kingly throne.

The low rays of the midafternoon sun lit up the makeshift burrow and put an end to Salem's nap. At first he welcomed the warmth, but when he opened his eyes and saw earthworm-plowed dirt around him instead of Sabrina's embroidered comforter, his mood soured. He flexed his claws into the sheepdog's belly, bringing Gotham to painful consciousness.

"Up and at 'em, Sleeping Booby," Salem grumbled. "Time to resume our new life of wandering down the road hopelessly searching for a way home. Unless we get lucky and Drell disintegrates us first."

The sheepdog effortlessly shifted from sleep to activity. He scrabbled out of the burrow, pummeling Salem with all four paws on the way. He stood in the middle of the path and, starting from his nose, gave himself a thorough wake-up shake. A moment later he was racing ahead and doubling back to prod his grumpy companion.

"C'mon, Salem!" Gotham barked. "Like you said, we gotta get going."

Salem slunk out of the burrow and reluctantly trotted ahead, pointedly ignoring Gotham as he capered from one side of the path to the other. More or less together, they followed the track out of the strange forest.

Gloom gave way to bright sunlight as the wood ended at the crest of a small hill. The dirt track continued winding down the slope toward an enormous farmstead composed of a dozen or more well-kept buildings sprawled around a large central house. Sheep munched fodder in sturdy pens, and distant mooing hinted at cattle in several of the barns. The entire complex was encirled by a wide canal, reminding Salem of medieval castles surrounded by moats. Like those castles, there was only one way across the "moat"—in this case, a wooden covered bridge, the entrance of which was their path's final destination.

"Who'd have guessed?" Salem remarked sourly. "Another farm."

Gotham screwed up his face as he studied the valley. "Looks like a big one. Take a lot of people to run it. Since we're way out in the boonies and there aren't any other houses nearby, they've gotta be commuters, because who'd want to live this far away from conveniences? That means there's a probably a Line station nearby."

Salem did a double-take at his canine companion, shocked nearly speechless. *"What?* Gotham, that was the most nearly intelligent thing I've ever heard you say. From whence comes this sudden brilliance?"

Gotham attempted a shrug. "I just thought about what you'd do."

"I see." With all of their involuntary closeness, Salem could only presume that some of his genius had rubbed off. A pleasant smugness crept over him. "Do tell me more about how much you've learned from my sterling example."

"Well, I just looked at the farm and tried to imagine you living on it. *Salem would hate it here,* I thought to myself. *He'd complain all the time— where's the satellite dish? Where's the pizza delivery? He'd want to run away every chance he could. And he'd rag everybody around him until somebody set up a Line station just to shut him up.* That's what I thought."

Salem blinked. "I'm honored . . . I think." He led the way down the hill to the covered bridge.

The bridge was a further sign that this was an extraordinary farm. Upon closer examination Salem saw that it was intensely rustic and picturesque, with a fresh coat of paint and well-kept shingling. But the planks of the floor were buried under a thick layer of scuffed soil, pocked with the tracks of shuffling sheep. Nobody who used this bridge worried about keeping their feet clean. Salem picked his way daintily through the dark tunnel, avoiding the muddier areas. *Gotham's right,* he thought. *I hate it here already.* His sheepdog companion pranced carelessly through the muck.

The bridge ended on the farm side with a small gate booth that interrupted the road. Two raccoons perched on the narrow counter of the booth's open service window, studying Salem and Gotham as they approached. Each raccoon clutched a clipboard loaded with thick stacks of paper, and their beady eyes glittered in their black-masked faces. As soon as the cat and dog stepped out of the covered bridge and into the light, the leftmost raccoon waved his hand.

With a squeal of rusted pulleys, a heavy gate woven of sticks and saplings slid down to block the bridge, sealing off retreat. The travelers spun around at the noise and spun right back again as the raccoons chittered enthusiastically.

"Look, Frick, we have *visitors!*" said the left raccoon, who was slightly fatter than the other.

"*Always* glad to have visitors, Frack, always glad," agreed the right raccoon, who was slightly taller than his partner. "Welcome, fellow animals! Welcome to the only place where animals are *truly* free!"

112

"Yeah, right," said Salem, acting much calmer than he felt. "If we're so welcome, what's with the gate?"

Frick dismissed the question with a wave of his paw. "Oh, that's just a precaution. A *precaution.* Lots of dangerous stuff in that woods, you know."

"'Can't be too careful' is *our* motto," added Frack.

Frick looked at Frack with some confusion. "I thought our motto was 'Don't ask *questions,* just follow *orders.'*"

"Being careful *is* following orders," Frack replied. He smiled at Salem and Gotham. "It's *our* job. What's *yours?*"

"We don't have jobs," Salem told them. "Unless you count being naturally graceful and decorative."

The two raccoons exchanged a worried glance. *"No jobs?"* they said in unison. "But what do you *do,* then?"

"I can't speak for the walking throw rug next to me"—Salem indicated Gotham—"but normally I eat as much as I can, sleep as much as I can, and do as little in return as possible. Right now, though, we're looking for a way back onto the Line."

Frick looked sharply at Frack. "Don't we have *orders* that say something about the Line?" Both raccoons rapidly shuffled through the paperwork on their clipboards.

"Got it!" exclaimed Frack. "Order 14326, part B. *Anyone who admits to knowledge of the Line or other witchcraft must be brought to the Leader's attention immediately.* You take their names, Frick, and I'll report them."

Frick frowned. "No way! You reported last time, Frack. Why do *I* have to get stuck with the *boring* part of the job?"

"You *do* have a point," admitted Frack. "The Leader says that all animals must share. Tell you what—we'll take their names *together.* Then *I'll* report the dog and *you* can report the cat."

Frick nodded. "Much better, *much* better."

"Deal." Frack turned back to Salem and Gotham. "Names?"

Salem didn't like the feel of this situation and kept mum. Unfortunately, Gotham was all too happy to be of service to the raccoons. "I'm Gotham and this is my pal Salem. We're lost."

Frick blinked. "Did you say Salem?"

"As in Saberhagen?" Frack asked, leaning forward with interest.

Too many strangers were interested in Salem today, and it disturbed him. "You know, guys," he began, slinking backward away from the booth, "we're running a little late, so I think my buddy and I will carry on our looking somewhere else. Nice to have met you and all that, but we really have to go."

Deep, menacing growls in stereo behind them halted all movement. Salem peeked ever so slowly over his shoulder. The gate was no longer the only obstacle to their departure. Two huge dogs, a pit

114

bull and an Irish wolfhound, stood before the gate, their heads low and their fangs bared. The pit bull's fierce grin was lopsided.

"Meet Broken Fang and Worrybone," chirped Frick. "They're our Special Visitor Escorts."

Salem summoned up all his cool and turned away from the terror dogs to smile insincerely up at the raccoons. "On the other hand," he said, "maybe we can stay for a *little* while longer."

Frick smiled back at him while Frack waved to a passing crow. The black bird dropped in a power dive, only pulling up at the last instant to land on the ledge next to the raccoon. Frack whispered urgently to the bird, then with an ugly "Skrawk!" the crow launched itself into the air again, making arrow-straight for the big farmhouse.

Frick indicated that Gotham and Salem should start walking. When they had passed the booth, the two masked rodents leaped aboard the guard dogs' backs, looking for all the world like fat jockeys in fur coats. Neither raccoon spoke again, except to call out turns for their "guests" to take. They alternated speaking, fastidiously dividing the work evenly between them.

Salem shifted his eyes from side to side as he walked, taking in every detail of this increasingly uneasy place. Humans were conspicuously absent, both by sight and by scent. The farm was unusually clean, and a strange silence hung over the place.

Cat and dog were led into the great farmhouse

and hustled down a hallway. Salem noted that the interior floors matched those of the covered bridge—nothing but scuffed dirt. Apparently brooms weren't in high demand in these parts. At the end of the hall was a sliding double door flanked by two different raccoons nearly identical to Frick and Frack. At the sight of the dogs, these raccoons tugged on their door handles, slipping the doors back into the wall only long enough to allow the escort dogs to butt their guests forward and through. Then the doors slammed shut again, nearly clipping Salem's tail and making Gotham jump.

Salem's fur bristled as he heard the doors *click* locked behind them.

☆

Chapter 14

☆

Sabrina and Noir stepped out of the Line and onto a steep hillside scored with narrow winding sheep walks. A sprawl of farm buildings filled the valley below. A small river had been diverted to surround the farmstead with a wide canal, rather like a moat, Sabrina thought. The only approach to the artificial island was by a wooden covered bridge.

A flock of crows rose up from the biggest barn and, most unnaturally, dissolved into pairs heading out in all directions. Noir grabbed Sabrina's sleeve and pulled her into the shelter of a bush. "I don't like the smell of this place," he growled in a low tone.

"Is Salem here?" was all Sabrina cared about.

"I don't catch his scent, or Gotham's. My guess is they're down there."

As far as Sabrina could tell, the farm appeared quiet and orderly. Dogs herded small bands of sheep down the hillsides to gather as one flock that filed through the covered bridge. *Lots* of dogs. Gotham had mentioned that dogs were holding Salem prisoner. Dogs and pigs. Curious, Sabrina conjured binoculars for a closer look.

The dogs nipping at the heels of the sheep looked like no country sheepdogs. Burly and stiff-coated, they looked more like canine thugs. They took obvious joy in driving the flock first one way and then another, keeping the sheep panicked and packed.

A pair of raccoons, perched atop a booth at the farm's end of the bridge, tallied the incoming sheep on clipboards clutched in their eerie little hands. A crow strutted behind them in the unmistakable attitude of a self-appointed supervisor.

Noir sniffed the air deeply. "That's odd," he said. "You're the only human that's been in this valley for a long time, but that farm doesn't look neglected."

"Looks positively guarded to me," Sabrina replied. "Check out the security patrols." She pointed toward the moat.

Pairs of dogs walked the water's edge at equal intervals. Each pair consisted of the same combination—a slender whippet and a massive pit bull.

"Chasers and Chompers," explained Noir. "One

to run it down, the other to overpower it. This place is wound tight as a hairball. You got a plan to get us in?"

"Me?" asked Sabrina in surprise.

Noir shrugged. "You made the deal—I track, you take care of trouble. You're on."

Sabrina straightened and studied the farm carefully. "Okay," she said, thinking aloud, "they don't look like the types to just let us stroll in and look around, so sneaking in is definitely called for. Zapping in would be the best way, but in a place I've never been before I could land us *inside* a wall. Bad thing, definitely. I'm afraid it's going to have to be a glamour—and I haven't practiced lately."

Noir looked blankly at her. "Is that some kind of fashion thing?"

"A witch thing, anyway," said Sabrina. "It's an illusion spell that changes how people see you. I'll make it so you look like a dog and I look like a cat and we'll mingle with the crowd heading in. I can't actually turn us into animals or I wouldn't be able to change us back. No fingers, no pointing—no magic!"

"Me, look like a dog again?" Noir said, shocked. "I dunno. . . . Wouldn't invisibility be better?"

"Well, I *could* make us invisible, but that wouldn't keep the dogs from smelling us. A glamour masks you completely. A dog and a cat it is, then." She raised her hands to commence the spell.

"Hold on, there, doll," Noir cautioned. "Don't go flying off the leash yet. You're forgetting something."

"What?"

"Those puppies down there," he said, indicating the patrolling dogs. "They'd *love* a cute kitty to play with. For a while, anyway."

Against her will, Sabrina had to agree that Noir was right. She didn't have to admit it, though. "Well, Sherlock," she demanded, "what does the great detective suggest?"

"Baaa."

Sabrina opened her mouth to refuse, but then reddened and shut it slowly. Noir was right again. But good grace was optional here, too. "I'm going to make sure you're an *ugly* dog," she said spitefully.

A whispered chant and several complex gestures later, a snow-white ewe bolted from the bush, escorted by a dog that could have been a littermate to the toughs working the other side of the valley. The dog loped down the hillside confidently, but the ewe seemed unsure of her footing until they joined the crush of sheep squeezing into the covered bridge.

Sabrina's glamours worked wonderfully for preventing hostile eyes from seeing anything but another dog and another sheep milling about, but they were no help at all in preventing human-shaped feet from being stepped on by sharp hooves. Sabrina's and Noir's feet were in jeopardy as long as the flock kept moving forward. Fortunately, the herd came to a halt at the gate booth where the two raccoons tried frantically to count sheep and record the numbers on clipboards. Mashed toes were less likely now, but the two disguised humans were stuck in the bottleneck.

The raccoons' work was made all the harder by the constant flow of crows carrying new orders and taking back rolled-up tally sheets. At first barely more than ugly squawking to Sabrina's ears, the crows' speech became more understandable the longer she remained a captive audience.

A new, larger crow swooped down from the skies, aggressively scattering its lesser kin from its desired perch above the raccoons. "Fresh orders! Fresh orders!" it cawed, strutting along the roof. "Listen to the Leader's words! Continue the gathering! Spies say the Hunting Lodge is hurt! The road is clear! Strangers are in the woods! No getting in— no getting out! Bring anyone suspicious directly to the Leader! Long live the Revolution!" Then, with a flutter of inky feathers, the crow was back in the sky, hurrying to take his message to other sentries.

The raccoons shrugged their shoulders at each other and bent back to their paperwork.

"Well, that takes care of backing out now," Noir whispered to Sabrina. "This place feels like a time bomb. We've got to get the straight scoop on what's going on. Can you cast a truth spell on those ring-tailed bandits so I can ask them some questions?"

"Truth sprinkles are the only spell I know that does that, and I don't have any," Sabrina whispered back. "But I did see Aunt Hilda do a *gossip* spell one slow day at the hairdresser's." She pointed her finger at the raccoons.

At once the leftmost raccoon glared up at the departed crow and chittered angrily, "The *nerve* of that crow! We are trained professionals, are we not, Frick? Like we don't know what to do in an emergency."

"One could *even* say that we wrote the book on it," Frick agreed, miffed.

"Parts of it," qualified his partner.

"Well, they were based on our *ideas.* . . ."

"Developed equally. Frick and Frack, back to back—"

"Share the credit and duck the blame!"

Frack frowned. "We've got to work on making that rhyme. Make a note of it."

Frick looked insulted. *"You* make a note of it!" he snapped. *"I'm* busy looking for infiltrators— *witches,* even!"

"And I'm *not?"* squealed Frack. "With the whole farm in a *tizzy* now that the road is clear—nasty, that Hunting Lodge, simply nasty—with Operation Underdog finally moving, you dare accuse *me* of shirking my job?"

"I never said *any* of that," Frick replied piously. "I merely pointed out that our *express orders* are to keep the border sealed so no word of the Leader's plans leak out. And since *my* job is to *follow* those orders, *you* have no right to try and distract me with irrelevant note-taking."

Sabrina missed Frack's retort as Noir whispered in her ear, "Something here stinks like day-old fish, and we're heading straight into the trash can."

"I don't care," Sabrina hissed back. "I'm not leaving here without Salem."

Noir stared at her. "You've got the loyalty of a dog. I admire that."

Their conversation was cut short by the arrival of two burly guard dogs. The newcomers reported in to the raccoons but maintained an attitude of really being the ones in charge. "Broken Fang and Worrybone, taking up station," the gap-toothed pit bull growled to Frick and Frack.

"Yeah," added the wolfhound. "We're also supposed to remind youse that it's yer turn to pick the Sheep of the Day fer tonight's banquet. Who's the lucky lamb?"

"Do you want them rated by offspring, milk production, or quality of fleece?" demanded Frick. "Or maybe the fattest?"

"Cleanest will do," snapped Broken Fang. "Sheep grease in the carpet puts a hurt on my nose."

"Delicate baby," sneered Worrybone. "Maybe

youse should transfer to the chicken detail—or do feathers make yer sneeze?" He began to snarl at the stocky dog.

"Keep it civil, pups," Frack threatened, "or we'll have to send your names to the Leader for *special attention.*" That distracted the dogs from their rivalry long enough for the raccoon to glance quickly over the herd and point at Sabrina. "Make it that one—she looks like she just took a bath."

The other sheep in the herd glanced at Sabrina with envy in their eyes. Sabrina wondered nervously what she was being picked for.

"You raccoons always get the cushy jobs," Broken Fang was muttering. "You pick and we get to do the work. Only it ain't gonna work that way today. We're on special alert, and this is our post. We ain't leaving."

"I'll take her," Noir said loudly.

Four pairs of eyes fixed him in their gaze. "Who are you?" they demanded in unison.

"The name's . . . Gnarr," the detective improvised. "I'm a new recruit and haven't gotten an assignment yet. Tell me where to take her and I'll get her there."

Everyone seemed relieved at this simple solution to a potentially annoying problem, even though Worrybone kept sniffing at Noir.

"Just take her up to the big house and tell Twisker she's to be kept clean till the award at dinner," instructed Frick.

"I don't understand how sheep can feel so proud of a silly loop of ribbon," said Frack. "But if a Sheep of the Day isn't picked like clockwork, the whole flock gets sulky. Sheep!"

Worrybone was taking a closer sniff at Noir's nose, so Noir quickly turned away and nipped at Sabrina's heels, driving her up toward the main farmhouse. "Blat or whatever it is that sheep do," he advised her in a whisper.

"Baaaaa!" Sabrina bleated. "Baa-baaa!"

"On second thought, don't."

Twisker proved to be a very old raccoon whose coat and mask had faded to the color of eddying smoke. His whiskers were so gnarled that if they were metal, they could have been corkscrews. He squatted on the door stoop of the main farmhouse and made a checkmark on his clipboard. "Sheep of the Day—Cleanest category." He turned to shout into the building. "Lop Ear! Tailstump! We've got a beauty queen today!"

Two huge dogs, bigger even than Broken Fang and Worrybone, trotted to the doorway. Obviously the household guard was made up of tougher troops than the patrols. Whoever ran this place took no chances about protection.

Noir bristled as the huge mongrels nosed Sabrina away from him and sent her skidding through the doorway. "Where are you taking her?" Noir growled.

"Like it's any of your business, newbie," Tailstump retorted. But his companion looked to Twisker for instructions.

The raccoon consulted his clipboard. "The Leader's having a banquet tonight, so lock her in Cell B until then."

"That okay by you, runt?" Tailstump asked Noir with a sneer that bared one yellow fang. When Noir made no reply, the dog said, "I thought so," and turned to drive Sabrina farther into the house and out of sight.

☆

Chapter 15

☆

Pet Noir Confidential Journal
The Case of the Wandering Boot

Dozens of plans raced through my head as Tailstump and Lop Ear led Sabrina away. I rejected all of them because of the risk involved to the angel. What irony! Thanks to the glamour spell, the world finally could see me in my true form—the shell of a dog who doesn't have the true dog strength to save a friend.

Moaning over soggy kibble never did anyone any good. I pulled myself back together and looked for a way to keep a close eye on the situation.

Nobody on the farm seemed to go anywhere alone. The dog patrols, the raccoons, even the crows traveled in pairs. The place ran like clockwork because everybody was poised to rat on everybody else. But that meant that my solo status would get me nailed, pronto. I had to find a partner.

I traded on my new identity as "Gnarr, the green recruit" and got a conceited whippet who called himself Windracer to volunteer as my personal tutor. Windy lived up to his name, taking me on an extensive tour of the grounds as we walked the perimeter along the moat. The more I heard, the less I liked leaving the doll alone with their beloved "Leader." It seemed he had some plans ready, in case a witch should drop out of the sky and into his trough.

I was seriously rethinking my obligations to Drell when Windy stopped me in my tracks.

"Ears up," he said. "Strangers coming through the bridge. Sneak up with me and listen." He turned to look me in the eye. "Just for security backup, you understand."

I nodded my agreement and invited him to take the lead. He thought I was deferring, but I was just protecting my cover—the cover I almost blew when I saw the strangers at the gate booth.

They were Salem and Gotham.

I cursed the fuzziness of time and space. My Line detector had taken me to the right place, but to the wrong time! We'd arrived too early!

I trembled with the urge to rush out and seize Gotham. My every instinct demanded that I catch my quarry. But I couldn't—Gotham *hadn't* left *yet to find us and make it possible for me to have tracked him here. If I arrested him now—interference from anybody else aside—he'd never get to leave to make me come here and find him.*

I hate paradoxes.

Sabrina wasn't worried when the door to the cell clicked shut. After all, it was only a sheep they were penning, and a closed door would do that easily. But the ace up this sheep's woolly sleeve was a wild card. Sabrina pointed a finger at herself to dissolve the glamour spell sheep disguise and turned the doorknob with a very human hand.

She conjured up a mirror and used it to make sure the hall was empty before stepping out of her cell. She frowned in thought. *Somehow I've got to find where Salem is being kept*—without *getting caught. I don't like those kind of odds.*

"Hey!" a weasely voice barked behind her. "Who let that sheep out of the cell?"

What sheep? thought Sabrina, confused.

A small black hand caught at the fabric of her trenchcoat and pulled her back toward the cell. "Let old Stickypaw get you back in here, lambkin," the annoyed raccoon murmured. "Then he has to find someone to put on report."

In a state of shock, Sabrina let the raccoon put her back in the cell. She caught her reflection in the polished surface of the door as it closed. A snowy ewe looked back at her. *Omigosh,* she thought. *The glamour didn't dissolve! I must have put too much endurance into the spell.*

Her heart sank as she heard a padlock being put on the door. Even if she used magic to get out again, everyone would still think she was a sheep— even Salem, if she was lucky enough to find him. Things were as bad as they could possibly be.

No, they're not, she realized. *I split that glamour spell between me and Noir. The Quizmaster is always warning me that spells are like equations. If my half of the spell is too strong, then Noir's half is too weak. His glamour might wear off at any minute!*

☆

Chapter 16

☆

As the double doors *snik*ed shut, Salem's mind flashed back to other desperate situations he'd survived. Of course, all those situations had been in movies or on TV and he'd been a comfortable spectator, but somewhere among them might be the key he needed to survive whatever horrible fate lay in store for him in this locked room.

His eyes scanned the room quickly, prepared to treat every object in it as a possible threat. He knew that in the hands of master villains, even common household furnishings could be put to deadly use. But if this was a torture chamber, he couldn't imagine how it worked.

It was a large room, with tall ceilings and windows that ran the full height of the walls. Velvet curtains covered the windows and blocked out the setting sun. One end of the room was filled by a luxurious spa with a large heated swimming pool and a mud tub. A hill of clean, fluffy towels filled the far corner, and from a hat rack a loop of blue denim dangled.

The other end held a banquet platform in front of an enormous fireplace. The centerpiece of the platform was a large, linen-draped trough flanked by smaller feed boxes. Benches warmed by the fire sat behind each of the settings, piled high with brocaded pillows. A huge cauldron of steaming mash bubbled merrily on an iron hook in the hearth.

Gotham, in typical dog fashion, ignored his surroundings in favor of simpler, more direct needs. He was already across the room and lapping thirstily from the swimming pool.

Without warning, the pool erupted. Like a breaching whale, a gunmetal-gray hog launched himself out of the pool, carrying with him a mountain of water. Gotham yelped and skittered backward, nearly colliding with Salem in his fright.

The hog clambered onto the pile of towels and rolled about until he was dry. Then he looked up at Salem and Gotham. "Care for a dip?" he said in a surprisingly cultured voice. "I find that it does wonders for the appetite."

Suddenly the doors burst open and a frantic racoon waddled in. He threw himself flat on his belly before the hog and pleaded, "A thousand pardons, Your Leadership! I had no idea you were already in here. The strangers should never have been allowed in without an escort!"

"Relax, Boswell," soothed the hog. "There was never any danger. Deimos and Phobos were here all the time."

At the mention of their names, two Doberman pinschers stepped out from behind window curtains. Their mouths gaped like they were smiling, but their flat eyes never left Salem and Gotham.

The hog beckoned to the raccoon. "Now come over here and make me respectable so I can greet my guests."

Boswell got to his feet, scampered up the hat rack as easily as a monkey, and snatched the blue band. He leaped from the rack to the hog's back and looped the cloth circle over the massive head to settle on his neck like a blue collar.

Feeling himself dressed now, the hog trotted toward the dining area, flapping one gray ear to invite Salem and Gotham to join him. "Don't you just love this place?" he said cheerfully. "It started out as a rustic playhouse for some Hollywood witches who had become overnight stars. They wanted a no-fuss farm to play Country Squire in, so they ordered state-of-the-Arts automagic control systems to run the place—you know the kind— self-filling pitchers, bottomless cornucopias, and the like."

The gray hog trundled up onto the bench behind the linen-draped trough. Boswell briskly tied a silk bib under the Leader's chin and directed Salem and Gotham to take the benches to the hog's right. When they had settled in, Salem next to the Leader and Gotham at the far end of the platform, the hog continued.

"Unfortunately for them, the critics hexed their next few pictures and they became instant has-beens. Everybody seemed to forget about us here at the farm, especially after the Hunting Lodge bloomed. We were left alone." Anger and a hint of dark frustration flashed across his face for the briefest of instants, masked by an earnest cheerfulness. "It proved to be a blessing in disguise, though. Animals learned that they didn't have to be dependent on two-leggers to get by. You might say it convinced us that almost anybody could run things better than they were being run." He leaned his enormous head down close to the black cat's. "A sentiment that you once believed in with all your heart," he said breathily. *"If* you're the real Salem Saberhagen."

"Oh, that's me, all right," the cat replied. "Unless you're mad at him, in which case I'm no relation at all."

The big pig rumbled with laughter. "Oh, droll," he gasped. "How very amusing. And what better proof of your identity? You must forgive me for being so discourteous to doubt you, but your arrival was so . . . timely, so . . . unanticipated, that I had to inquire personally. I do hope you'll forgive me."

"Sure, you're forgiven," said Salem. "Whoever you are."

The hog reared back suddenly, stung with contrition. "Oh, I am such a poor host! We totally skipped introductions. I'm Steely Joe, humble hog and, by overwhelming popular choice, beloved Leader of our valiant little community." He shrugged his fatty shoulders. "Well, someone had to fill the power vacuum. And you're the famous Salem Saberhagen. I'm your biggest fan. I followed your trial every day on HEX-TV." Steely Joe rapped manicured trotters on the trough. "Boswell! The scrapbook!"

The fat raccoon trundled up to the platform with a stack of newspaper clippings bound between leather covers. "I researched your career in minute detail, dear boy," Steely Joe said. He smiled over at Gotham. "Your friend was the center of the Trial of the Century—maybe of the Millennium. He could have had a place in the Tyrant's Hall of Fame." He smiled sympathetically at Salem. "Except you got caught first. And then, defeated, humiliated, all your hopes dashed, you voluntarily gave up your two-legged status and became an animal."

"It was the only choice Drell offered me that wasn't painful or instantly fatal," snorted Salem. "You can ask him," he added, indicating the sheepdog with a flick of his tail. "He was there."

"You were?" cooed Joe. "And who might you be, my shaggy lad?"

Gotham sat up straight, his tail wagging like a windmill. "I'm Gotham. I'm Salem's friend and boon companion. I'm helping him find a way back onto the Line, so he can put the Boot in its proper place." He shook his chest to make the sandal swing. "We have a plan."

Steely Joe literally fell off his bench with a bang. His eyes widened and darted from Salem to the Boot and back again. "The Boot . . . a plan . . ." he muttered. Emotions flashed over his bristled face. He stared at Salem as the room suddenly filled up with guard dogs and fat scout rats, all drawn by the unexpected noise.

Without taking his eyes from the cat's, Steely Joe held up a trotter. With the exception of a couple of crows who flew in late, everyone in the hall froze instantly. Echoing in the hushed room, Steely Joe clambered back onto the bench and demanded hoarsely, "You know how to activate the power of the Boot? And you came here?" His voice slid into a deadly whisper. "Are you launching a takeover again?"

Salem looked nervously around the room. Sharp claws, dripping fangs, and unfriendly eyes were everywhere. He wished with all his might that Gotham be struck by a bolt of lightning. His mind raced for an answer that wouldn't blow up in his face. "No comment."

Steely Joe exhaled slowly. "I see," he murmured. The room relaxed as he did. He pursed his lips at Salem. "Join me for dinner?"

Salem struggled to keep calm. "Sounds cool. We'll have whatever you're having."

"Splendid!" Joe said, and tapped his trough twice.

A squadron of raccoons and rats scurried to the hearth, splitting into teams to pull chains and ropes to pivot the bubbling cauldron out into the room. Two raccoons used long sticks to tip the rocking cauldron forward, pouring a river of hot mash into Steely Joe's trough. Rat teams carried Salem's and Gotham's smaller troughs like pallbearers to be filled up at the iron pot with a couple of deft tilts. As a final trough was filled, an escort detail ushered a snowy-white ewe into the hall. The trough and the ewe were placed to Steely Joe's left.

The Leader sat up straight on his bench and explained to the visitors, "Before we begin our meal, it is customary to present awards. They are tokens of the value of each and every member of our community. They raise the morale of the common folk here on the farm. And, since the sheep usually eat them, they are a fine addition of nutritious fiber to their diets."

Raccoons ceremoniously drew the curtains back from the tall windows. Outside, sheep pressed up against the glass to watch one of their own being honored. Old Boswell trundled forward and hung a blue ribbon around the ewe's neck, proclaiming, "Behold, this day's Sheep of the Day! Let's hear it for a clean fleece. May you all strive to outdo her!"

The windows were covered again and the Leader shouted, "Dig in!" He wasted no time thrusting his snout into the mash and *shlurp*ing down.

Salem took a few delicate bites of the grain porridge just to be polite, noticing that Gotham slurped the stuff up enthusiastically while the ewe didn't touch hers. Instead, she stared fixedly at Salem. Something about the sheep seemed familiar to him, but he couldn't quite place it.

He had no time to learn sheep body language, though. Thanks to Gotham's big mouth, getting back on the Line seemed impossible, and even getting out of this room might be difficult. He needed more information. "So, it's nice to meet a fan," he said. "Do you want my pawprint in your scrapbook?"

"I will be honest with you, tyrant to tyrant. I, too, have plans for world conquest. I wish to right the wrongs done to animals throughout the Other Realm. Daily I brood on ways of overthrowing the oppressive rule of the two-legged and replacing it with my own benevolent dictatorship. I am a hog with a dream, a hog of destiny." He tapped his trotters together and the guard dogs all came to attention. In unison they drew closer, except for one very wobbly dog near the back. "I am also a hog with a secret army." He smiled. "Then you arrive—my role model, the fellow who almost made it, bringing with you the very tool to make my dreams reality! You will tell me freely or you will tell me painfully, but you will tell me truly— how do you unleash the king-making power of the Boot?"

Chapter 17

☆

Salem looked at the brutal canine faces surrounding him and swallowed hard. "I can't," he croaked.

"You can't," repeated Steely Joe with obvious disbelief. "Then why did you steal it from Drell's Treasury, where I know it was stored?"

"I *didn't* steal it," Salem wailed plaintively. He waved a paw at Gotham, who lifted his mush-covered muzzle at their attention. *"He* did, thinking it would help me go back into world conquest again. So *he* could have *fun!"* He turned back to Steely Joe and tried to explain. "But it was pointless from the start—I can't tap its power. *None* of us can."

Steely Joe dropped his genteel folksiness and turned red under his gray coat. "You *lie!"* he hissed. "It is the greatest weapon in Drell's arsenal. It makes his will stronger—strong enough to overpower all resistance."

Salem shrugged his shoulders. "That's the PR. And it works, too. But only for a *witch*. It amplifies a witch's natural power. Ex-witches and powerless animals need not apply."

The Leader barked commands. "Boswell—fetch me the Boot. Deimos, Phobos—make sure he cooperates!"

The two fierce dogs leaped onto the platform and pinned Gotham between them. Their alpha dominance intimidated the poor witch-turned-sheepdog as much as their snarls and bared teeth. The fat raccoon pulled the sandal's thong over Gotham's head and carried it carefully back to Steely Joe.

The hog hung the Boot from one trotter, swinging it before Salem's panicked eyes. "Now, cat, you will tell me the truth of this thing's operation, or a thousand fangs will persuade you."

Gotham shrieked, a heart-rending, sorrowful sound. "I'm sorry, Salem! I only wanted to help you!" A light came into his eyes. "That's it! I'll go for help!"

The guard dogs shifted to block his way out of the room, but to their surprise, Gotham spun around and leaped directly at the solid brick fireplace behind him. He disappeared an inch before hitting the bricks, filling the hall with a deep *bong*ing noise.

"Where did he go?" shrilled Steely Joe, nearly deafening Salem.

"He might be anywhere," Salem replied helplessly. "He seems to be able to travel the Line at will."

"The Line?" Steely Joe's eyes bulged. "The *Line!* First you lie to me when you tell me the Boot is useless. Then you lie to me by not telling me that your friend could open the Line for me and my troops to take the entire Other Realm by surprise! For this you will die slowly and very painfully!"

"No, he won't!" a voice shouted from the crowd of dogs facing the banquet. A cloudy-looking dog leaped forward, its shape shredding as it moved until it was clearly a human form that snatched the Boot from the Leader's trotter with a five-fingered hand. The last of the glamour spell dissolved around Pet Noir as he stood between Salem and the rest of the room.

The cat gaped at his rescuer. "Noir!"

"I told you I'd track you down, cat." Noir shouted at Steely Joe's minions. "You're all under arrest! Freeze them, Sabrina!"

If Salem was surprised to see Noir coming to his aid, he was flabbergasted to hear Sabrina's voice answer from the white ewe's mouth.

"I can't," she bleated. "I made my glamour too strong and I can't break it to use my magic properly!"

Noir looked from Sabrina-the-sheep to the room

full of foes. In one fluid move, he snatched up a fire iron from the hearth and threw the Boot over Steely Joe's head to Sabrina. As soon as the sandal was airborne, he gripped the iron with both hands and positioned himself to defend Salem.

As she caught the Boot, Sabrina yelled, "What am I supposed to do with it?"

"You're a witch!" Salem hollered back. "Put it on to increase your power!"

So solid was the sheep illusion that Sabrina couldn't be sure where her feet actually were. Instead, she slipped her hand into the worn leather.

Immediately she felt a supernatural rush of confidence and an instant grasp of the power of command. A flick of her newly bolstered will shattered the stubborn spell disguise and drew the attention of every animal in the room to the suddenly visible witch girl. Not even a ghost of fear dimmed her confidence. Sabrina held the Boot out at arm's length and commanded loudly, "Go away!"

As a magical device, the Boot had gained its power from being in close contact with iron-willed fighters. It strengthened the true power of its wielder rather than creating new power. Sabrina was a novice witch, still training for her Witch License. All the Boot could help her do was sway the less fanatical animals in the room.

All of the rats and raccoons bolted first, then all of the confused or weak dogs. Unfortunately, Steely Joe and his personal guard dogs remained strong-willed enough to resist Sabrina's command. Deimos and Phobos snarled and danced closer to Salem and Noir, while Steely Joe turned to bring his baleful gaze on the teenage girl-witch.

"Get away, doll!" yelled Noir, pulling out his Line detector. "I'll get us out through the Line!" Deimos leaped at the detective's arm, snapping fiercely. Blood spattered and the Line detector toppled into the fire from a ripped hand. Noir shoved the giant dog back, but his gadget was already melted plastic. "Get out of here!" he ordered Sabrina. "I'll hold them off as long as I can!"

The snarling dogs sensed the detective's weakness and closed in on him.

Steely Joe extended a trotter toward Sabrina. "Give me the Boot, girl. Your friends are no match for my alpha warriors."

The Leader's words sparked a memory in Sabrina's head—something that Noir had said about alpha males. An idea blossomed in her mind and she pointed the Boot at the trapped Noir.

Summoning all her strength, she chanted,

*"You gave up a body to work for Drell.
I command the Boot to break that spell!"*

Flashes of energy crackled around Noir's body, thickening it until it burst the seams in his trenchcoat. His back stooped and his face grew long and fierce. Drell had forced Noir to choose between his animal form and his human form, but both were his by rights. In seconds, the human-shaped Pet Noir transformed into his alter self, the wild son of the Alpha of Alphas in the North.

Noir's daddy may have been an alpha male, but a good deal of his power came from the fact that he was also a primeval Dire Wolf, an ancient breed that went head to head with saber-toothed tigers— and won. Recognition of his dominance was bred into the very genes of lesser canines, even those as fierce as Lop Ear and Tailstump or Deimos and Phobos. The dogs contiued to growl and snap, but they retreated slowly out the door.

If Steely Joe had been a boiler, his pressure would have been redlining right then. But even he had to bow before the combined force of the Dire Wolf and the witch with the Boot. Surrounded by his retreating troops, he edged his way out the double doors, but before he slammed them shut, he screamed, "We have you surrounded by hundreds of my loyal troops. You cannot hold out here forever. You are doomed!"

The slamming of the doors echoed in the ears of Sabrina, Salem, and Noir the Dire Wolf. The Leader was right. Without the Line detector, they were trapped.

Then the room *bong*ed.

☆

Chapter 18

☆

The world contracted around Sabrina, narrowing to a bubble in a tube. Other bubbles jostled hers as they twisted and turned in their race down the tube. An instant later she found herself in open air in front of a monumental staircase leading up to a set of massive gold double doors. A familar *bong*ing still rang in her ears.

Monstrous gargoyles leered out from every rampart of the enormous building. Warning runes carved deeply into the walls advised, "I'd turn back if I were you." Richly embroidered tapestries hung on either side of the door bore appliquéd letters saying GO AWAY.

"Welcome to Drell's Treasury," Salem announced. Sabrina hadn't realized that her cat was nearby until he'd spoken. She snatched him up in her arms, cradling him against the Boot, which she still held.

Salem squirmed against the public display of affection. "Can we save this for later? We've got company."

Sabrina finally noticed Gotham and Pet Noir standing on the steps beside them. Noir was slowly shifting back into his human form, complete with trenchcoat and hat, while Gotham looked from face to face to face, searching for approval for his rescue effort. She smiled at him, which made him blush and look away.

The steps leading up to the door were carved from living red velvet. The banister was carved from what looked like solid pearl. Gotham sighed as he began to climb. "Boy, I just love these stairs!"

Through her shoes, Sabrina couldn't feel anything special, but Salem squirmed to get down. Once on the carpet, he flexed his toes, digging deep into the soft pile. "Feel good?" Sabrina asked him, amused.

"Heavenly," the cat rumbled. "I could walk up and down these all day! Or nap on them. Or better yet, claw them!"

Noir said nothing.

The quartet reached the landing and found themselves standing before a set of double doors that opened onto a high-screened gallery overlooking the wealth of Drell's Treasury. More like a city than a warehouse, it was so big and so crammed with *stuff* that Sabrina couldn't see the far walls. *How in the world does Drell find anything here?* she wondered.

"This is just the viewing gallery," said Gotham. "The main levels are down below." He trotted over to a travel tube, which looked like a transparent elevator, and hopped inside. "C'mon!"

A minute later all three of them were in the tube, dropping like stones. Sabrina expected her stomach to protest, but aside from a slight vibration under her shoes, she felt nothing. They reached floor level and the transparent door slid open.

The treasury was amazing—shelves upon shelves of knickknacks, statues, books, trinkets, and baubles, all glittering with gems, gold inlay, or inherent magical powers. Sabrina gasped. Salem's knees went weak.

Gotham just calmly trotted forward, heading down one bogglingly long aisle that held nothing but what looked like lounge tikis—carved wooden figures sprinkled with glitter and draped with pukka shells and other disco jewelry. Sabrina and the others followed the dog, wondering at the strange junk around them. They reached the end of the aisle, and Gotham disappeared around the corner.

Sabrina followed, and her eyes bulged. Around the corner towered a huge refrigeration unit, and behind its frosty doors were the most outrageous items she could ever imagine: a replica of the

Sphinx done in chopped liver; an alarmingly life-like ice sculpture of Skippy the Overlord's Underling, grinning and holding up a frosty sign reading ICE TO MEETCHA!; even a full-sized velociraptor frozen in midleap. *I hope there's never a power failure here,* Sabrina thought, shivering.

Gotham was still moving, leaving Sabrina and Salem to scurry and catch up. Noir padded along effortlessly behind them.

Gotham reached the start of another aisle, but instead of heading down it, he stopped at a mahogany display case containing a single ivory shelf. On that shelf sat a delicate glass box. On that box nestled an empty velvet cushion—the Boot's original resting place.

Salem watched in disbelief as Gotham turned expectantly to Sabrina. She handed him the Boot, which the dog took in his mouth. Then he reared up on his hind legs and laid the battered slab of leather down on the cushion. Noir, who hadn't intruded himself onto the scene until now, breathed a sigh of relief.

"I hate to admit it," Salem said under his breath, "but it's probably better off here."

Gotham grinned, but under his bangs his eyes were a little sad. "I stole it for you, Salem, but the fact is, dominating the world was your dream, not mine. I only wanted to travel to new places and see new things. I don't need the Boot to do that—you showed me how to do it by surfing the Line." The sadness in his eyes turned into a gleam of excitement. "With the Line, I can spend the rest of my life just wandering from place to place. You've always treated me better than anybody else, Salem, and you saved my life from the Hunting Lodge. I'll always owe you for that, but . . . but the Line is my home now."

The air *bong*ed as Gotham opened up a portal to the Line. He looked at Salem and Sabrina. "Thanks for all the fun." He looked over at Noir. "You coming?"

Sabrina turned to the detective. "You're leaving, Noir?"

A struggle crossed Noir's face, shifting it from human to wolf and back again. "Call me Pet," he said softly. Shrugging, he reached into his breast pocket and took out the leather folder that held his security badge, tossing it down next to the leather sandal. "Tell Drell he's gonna need a new watchdog. I quit."

Noir stepped close to Sabrina and took her hand in his, gazing down at her with an almost puppylike sincerity. "Someday, doll, after all this madness is over, maybe we can find some time together, just you and me. A beach, or better yet, a park—someplace to get away from this life of endless dogged pursuit. We can play Frisbee."

Sabrina grinned at the young man with his rumpled hair sticking out from under his battered fedora. "Sounds like fun," she said.

Noir nodded once, tugged the brim of his hat by way of salute, and stepped back into the rift Gotham still held open.

"Good riddance!" Salem said.

"As for you, cat—" Noir glared at Salem.

"Uh, we had a deal, didn't we, Noir—I mean, Pet?" Sabrina ventured.

"Don't worry, doll. If there's one thing this case has taught me, it's to not pay too much attention to circumstantial evidence. It's obvious the kitty isn't a threat without that criminal mastermind to cover for him." He disappeared into the Line, shifting into wolf form, and the rift closed after him.

Sabrina heard a long, almost sad sigh, and realized it had come from her. *Frisbee,* she thought, and giggled. "Well, I guess it's time to go, Salem," she said, starting back for the tiki aisle. "Hilda and Zelda will be happy you're home. They may even fix you some tuna surprise as a . . ." She stopped, realizing Salem was not following.

He was still sitting in front of the ivory display case, glowering at the place where Noir had disappeared. "What did he say? Criminal mastermind?" Salem snorted. *"Gotham?"* Then the insult sunk in. "Hey, what did he mean, the kitty's *not a threat?* I could show him—"

"In your dreams, cat!" Sabrina said, scooping him up in her arms. "Forget conquering the world. You can't open a can of food without help."

About the Authors

David Cody Weiss and Bobbi JG Weiss are a husband and wife writing team. They're big fans of Sabrina, the Teenage Witch and have written a number of novels for the series including *#3 Good Switch, Bad Switch, #8 Salem on Trial* and *#13 Go Fetch!* They have also written animation, comic books and a trilogy of films that never got made! David and Bobbi live in the USA.